"I'm willi

whatever wa

success."

low

A wry smile curved his wicked mouth. He wasn't fooled by her display of calm, and that made her angry. That he could see through her. That he was amused by her.

Ella extended her hand and he grasped it. Lightning shot through her, unexpected, instant, as if she'd touched a naked wire. It mingled with the anger, the adrenaline that was already pounding through her, and made her feel shaky, as if her knees might give out at any moment.

She looked up and met his eyes, and saw heat. Attraction. He looked down at where their hands were joined, his large and dark, hers small and pale. And marred. He ran his thumb over one of the scars that blazed a jagged path over the back of her hand.

The heat fled, leaving in its place an icy shiver that made her feel cold inside. She pulled her hand from his grasp.

His gaze lingered on her. "It will be a pleasure doing business with you."

Maisey Yates was an avid Mills & Boon® Modern™ Romance reader before she began to write them. She still can't quite believe she's lucky enough to get to create her very own sexy alpha heroes and feisty heroines. Seeing her name on one of those lovely covers is a dream come true.

Maisey lives with her handsome, wonderful, diaper-changing husband and three small children across the street from her extremely supportive parents and the home she grew up in, in the wilds of Southern Oregon, USA. She enjoys the contrast of living in a place where you might wake up to find a bear on your back porch and then heading into the home office to write stories that take place in exotic urban locales.

THE
HIGHEST PRICE
TO PAY

BY
MAISEY YATES

First published in Great Britain 2011
by Mills & Boon, an imprint of Harlequin (UK) Limited,
Eton House, 18-24 Paradise Road, Richmond, Surrey TW9 1SR

© Maisey Yates 2011

ISBN: 978 0 263 88682 5

Harlequin (UK) policy is to use papers that are natural, renewable and recyclable products and made from wood grown in sustainable forests. The logging and manufacturing process conform to the legal environmental regulations of the country of origin.

Printed and bound in Spain
by Blackprint CPI, Barcelona

THE
HIGHEST PRICE
TO PAY

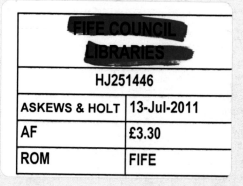

For Jenny, my editor.
Your confidence in me is always inspiring.
You've pushed me to become a better writer,
and you can't know how much that means to me.
And for my husband, Haven.
There's a little bit of you in all my heroes.

CHAPTER ONE

"This is it?" The man, tall dark and handsome as sin, who had just walked into Ella's small boutique gave his surroundings a dismissive glance.

She forced a smile. "Yes. All of the clothing here in the boutique is a part of the Ella Stanton line, and at the moment everything is quite scaled back as we're working on a…" *budget.* "Local level."

The fashion industry wasn't a cheap one to operate in, and Ella was most definitely still working her way up. But she was able to have her line produced, and sell it in her own boutique, and that certainly wasn't a small feat.

"I was merely curious," he said, taking a step toward her, "about my most recently acquired assets."

Ella blinked. "And by that you mean?"

"The Ella Stanton label, and the boutique, such as it is." His voice was smooth, husky as though he were issuing some kind of practiced pickup line, even though what he was really saying was far too ridiculous to be true. And yet, there was something else there, a hardness that lingered just beneath that suave accent. It was a hardness, an authority, that made all of the words that were swirling in her head get caught in her throat.

He took a step toward her and recognition punched

her in the stomach with brutal force. Blaise Chevalier. Rogue investor, ruthless corporate raider and tabloid superstar. He was famous in Paris or, rather, infamous. Wealthier than Midas, beyond handsome with his deep mocha skin, and striking toffee-colored eyes, perfect bone structure, good enough to be a model, except he didn't possess the androgynous quality many male models did. No, Blaise was utterly masculine, tall and broad shouldered with a physique that was meant to be wrapped in an expensive, custom-made suit.

She should have recognized him immediately. Her only excuse was that mere photographs simply didn't do him justice. Three dimensional, in the flesh, he was something entirely different than he was in the paper. None of the carefree, playboy demeanor was present now. Just a dark intensity that made her insides tremble, a sensual energy that no photograph would ever be able to capture.

He reached into his jacket pocket and took out a thin stack of folded papers. It wasn't cheap, bright white printer paper like she used in her office. This was cream colored, thick and textured. Official looking. A tremor skated down her spine and she shook it off, straightening her shoulders and holding out her hand.

He gave her the documents and stood there looking at her, his expression impossible to read. Ella looked down at the papers in her hand, skimming them frantically. Her stomach sank to her toes and the words blurred slightly.

"Would you mind translating? I'm not fluent in lega-lese," she said, hoping her voice didn't sound as echoey and distant to him as it did to her.

"Bottom line? I am now the lien holder on your business loan. A sizable amount."

She felt her face get hot, the way it always did when she thought of the screaming amount of debt she'd gotten in to get her business off of the ground.

"I'm aware of that. How did this…happen?" If it had been anyone else, she simply wouldn't have believed them. But she knew this man, even if it was only by reputation. And it wasn't a good thing that he was here with bank documents that possessed both the name of her business and the stark truth of just how little actually belonged to her.

"The bank that originally held your loan has been bought out by a larger financial institution. They auctioned off most of the small business loans, including yours. I bought your loan in a bundle with several others that are of much greater interest to me."

"So you own my business…and I'm uninteresting?" Ella pushed her blond hair off her face and sat down in one of the chairs reserved for her boutique customers.

"That's the summation."

It didn't get worse. It couldn't. And at that moment she just wanted to fall to her knees and scream at the sky. Because hadn't she been through enough? How much was she expected to overcome in her lifetime?

Blaise Chevalier had a reputation as a man who was self-indulgent, reckless and ruthless enough to betray his own brother in the coldest way imaginable. He crushed companies, large or small, if they passed into his sphere of power and he deemed them to be unprofitable.

And he was now the owner of her boutique, her workshop, her apartment…everything down to her sewing machines. Everything in her life that meant anything.

"And what's your conclusion?" she asked, standing again. She wasn't going to crumble. Not now. Not when the stakes were so high. Her career, her line, it was her life. It was everything she'd worked so hard to achieve, a dream she wasn't about to let go of now, not while she still had some hope.

"I'm in the business of making money, Ms. Stanton. And your boutique and clothing line are not making enough to cover the expense of running them and earn you a decent living."

"They will. I need a couple of years. By then, with some extra advertising I'll have built a larger client base and I can start doing the bigger runway shows, getting broader exposure."

He raised one dark brow. "And then?"

"And then…" She took a deep breath. She knew this. She had everything planned down to what color her dress would be at Fashion Week. "Then Paris Fashion Week, New York, Milan. More boutiques picking up my collection. I hope to have a retail line. I have it all in a portfolio if you'd like to see it. It's my five-year plan."

He had the gall to look bored, disinterested. "I don't have five years to wait for a venture to pay out. And as a result you don't have five years, either."

A hot shot of anger infused her with much-needed adrenaline. "What do you want me to do, march up and down the boulevard with a sandwich board strapped to my chest to drum up enough business to satisfy you? These things take time. Fashion is a very competitive industry."

"I was thinking something a bit more high-end, something with more…class." The slight curl of his lips suggested he didn't think she possessed any class at all.

She scrunched her curls, curls she knew were a little bit disheveled. That was the idea. She didn't do anything by accident, not even things that looked accidental. Everything, down to her spiky heeled, open-toed boots, was about her image and her business. Was about cultivating interest in her brand.

"Well, you weren't talking class, you were talking urgency."

"I thought you might be after a slightly more upscale clientele as opposed to tourists and backpackers," he said, his rich, slightly accented voice sending a shiver through her. Stupid. She talked to a lot of French men who were looking for clothing for their wives or girlfriends...or themselves, she should be used to the smooth charm of the accent by now.

For some reason it sounded different coming from him, a harder edge to complement the rounded vowels. His English was tinged with French, but also with another flavor she couldn't place, something that made his speech all the more exotic and fascinating.

It didn't change the fact that he had walked into her boutique like he owned the place and then proceeded to tell her that, in effect, he did.

"What's the point of advertising at all if you're just going to demand that I pay you back with money I haven't got?" she asked.

"I didn't say I was going to do that. I said that I expect you to start turning major profits in much less than five years' time."

"Have a magic wand in that briefcase?" She knew how to handle people like him, people who exercised control over others. Never show fear. Never show weakness. A hard-learned lesson, one she carried with her, always.

"I don't need magic," he said, his full lips curving slightly.

No, she imagined he didn't. He wasn't only famous for being the bad boy of the business world, he was famous for making millions just a few years after leaving his father's investing firm and stepping out on his own.

More than once, when she was struggling to make a loan payment, she'd seen an article about him in the business section of the paper and wondered how in the world he'd done it. Gone off on his own like that and made an almost instant success out of himself.

"Fairy dust?" she asked, crossing her arms beneath her breasts.

"Only the weak need luck and magic," he said. "Success comes to those who act, to those who make things happen."

Things like shutting down businesses and wrecking what *Style* magazine had called the wedding of the century. No secret that Blaise Chevalier made things happen, things that served him well. And that he did it with absolutely no conscience.

"And what exactly do you want to make happen with *my* company?" she asked, feeling her stomach tighten.

She was at a loss. She was going to lose control of her business, at best. At worst she would lose it entirely and if that happened, what was left?

No workshop. No boutiques. No industry parties. None of the friends she'd made thanks to the meager status that she'd achieved. It was like standing on the edge of an endless chasm staring down into nothing. The void was so dark, so empty. She'd crawled her way out of there once, and she couldn't go back. She wouldn't sink back down into oblivion, into nothing. She wouldn't let them be right about her.

"I'll admit, the fashion industry is of very little interest to me. But when I purchased the loan bundle from your financial institution, yours came wrapped up with what I actually wanted. A little research has shown me that it is time for me to pay more attention to the fashion industry, perhaps. It's much more lucrative than I had thought."

"If you play your cards right, yes, there's a lot of money to be made," she said. Although, massive amounts of money had never been what it was about for her. It was the success.

"Yes, if you play your cards right. But you're not exactly a master of the game. I, however, am." He moved closer to her, ran his hand along the carved wooden back of the chair she'd been sitting in earlier. She took a step back, strangely aware of the movements of his fingers over the intricate carving, almost like he was touching her, not the chair. Her heart pounded a little bit faster.

"I'm hardly a novice. I went to school for business and design. I have a business plan and a couple of investors."

"Low-level investors that lack the proper connections or sufficient funding. You need more than that."

"What do I need?"

"Publicity and cash and your five-year plan becomes a six-month plan."

"That's not even…"

"It is, Ella. I can have you at Paris Fashion Week next year, and in that time frame your work will have graced magazine covers, billboards. Selling your own work in your own boutique is one thing, but having worldwide distribution and recognition is another. I can give you that."

She could feel the reins slipping out of her fingers, feel herself losing control. She gritted her teeth. "In return for what? My eternal soul?"

A short chuckle escaped his lips. "While it has been

reported that I may be missing my own soul, I have no interest in yours. This is about money."

It was about more than that for her. Money was money. She could make money doing a lot of different things. But this, this was about being something. Being someone. She didn't want to have this man, anyone, so involved in her business, so involved in her achievements.

She didn't want it, but she wasn't stupid.

The amount of money she owed, money that was now owed to him, was staggering. More than she could hope to pay back with the way things stood. She was in debt to him up to her Petrova diamond earrings and if she ever hoped to get out of that debt, her business had to succeed. More than succeed, it had to reach the kinds of heights that, at the moment, were firmly in the realm of fantasy.

"You think you can just dictate to me?"

"I know I can. As the lien holder I have to be satisfied that you're doing everything in your power to ensure the success of your business. I'm not overly convinced at the moment," he said, his eyes sweeping the small boutique in a dismissive manner.

As if it were nothing. As if she were nothing. Her stomach burned with emotion, anger, helplessness. Fear. She hated the fear most of all. In theory she'd gotten over being afraid of bullies a long time ago.

"What if I don't want you running *my* business for me?" she asked, despising the slight quiver in her voice. She wasn't some scared little mouse and she wouldn't behave like one. She'd endured worse than this, and she'd triumphed. She would do it now, too.

"Then I pull the plug. I don't have the time to waste

on a venture that isn't going anywhere, and it's not in my nature to simply sit back."

"But you'll be collecting interest on your investment won't you?"

"Twenty-five percent," he said.

"Highway robbery," she responded, her voice finding some of its strength.

"Not in the least. I will be working for that money, and I will expect you to do the same."

"And you expect me to do as you say?"

He gripped the back of the chair, his large hands drawing her attention again. His appearance was so together, so perfectly polished that it would be easy to assume he was a civilized man. But beneath all of that, beneath the well-fitted suit and hand-crafted Italian shoes that were so gorgeous they gave her heart palpitations, was a hardness that betrayed him. A hardness that spoke of the ruthlessness that he was so famous for. That let her know he wouldn't hesitate to pull everything out from under her if it was in his best interest.

"Consider yourself lucky, Ella. Normally I would charge a hefty hourly fee to give out business advice. In this scenario, unless you make money, you don't give me any money. This is fair, more than fair."

She blinked rapidly. "Are you expecting me to thank you for this hostile takeover?"

"It's not hostile at all. It's business. I invest where it is advantageous to do so, I do not waste time when it's not. There is a place for charity, and this is not it."

Ella looked around her carefully organized boutique, at the racks of clothing, each one her own design. She'd painted the crisp black and white walls herself, had installed the glossy marble floor with the help of a couple of male models who'd done runway shows for her. It was personal to her, there was no way she could reduce all of her hard work to numbers and projections. But he'd done it.

And he would do more than that. Even without his reputation she wouldn't doubt him. The glint of fire in his golden eyes and the firm set of his angular jaw told her that he was not a man to be taken lightly.

"You're quite into the party scene, aren't you?"

Blaise watched as Ella stiffened, her bubblegum-pink lips tightening into a firm line. She didn't like his assessment of her. She didn't like his presence full stop, that much was clear.

But she could hardly deny that when her picture made it into the paper, it was because she was at some high profile soiree. It seemed she went to any and every event in Paris, at least those she could gain admittance to. And, from what he'd discovered, there were spare few she couldn't. A gorgeous American heiress with a sensational, tragic backstory was always in demand. And she took advantage of that.

"It's called promo, weren't we discussing that earlier?" she asked, arching one finely groomed brow.

Yes, she was beautiful, fine bone structure, bright blue eyes overly enhanced now by a thick line of blue pencil drawn all the way around them, making them look wider, more cat-shaped. It was obvious that she had no problem drawing attention to herself. She was wearing a short black dress that displayed her long, shapely legs to perfection, and ornate ankle boots with buckles and a cutout at the toe that showed off shockingly pink toenails.

A sharp shot of lust stabbed at his stomach. He dismissed it. This wasn't about lust; this was about business.

He'd learned long ago to separate the two. Learned never to let desire lead him around like a dog on a leash.

"It's ineffective," he said sharply. "Yes, it gets your name in the paper to go to every night club opening in Paris, but it's not elevating you to the level this boutique suggests you want to be at."

"At this point, I just need to get my name in the paper. I do what I can to drum up interest in the Ella Stanton label."

"You don't do enough."

"Thank you," she said, her tone flat.

"It cheapens you."

Her blue eyes widened. "It isn't as though I'm out engaging in questionable activities, you make it sound like I'm dancing on tables while shouting the name of my label. I always behave in a professional manner."

"You have to surround yourself with potential clients. Tell me, are any of those hard-partying patrons of the events you frequent going to come and spend money on your clothes?"

"Some of them…"

"Not enough of them. You need to build connections in the industry. You need to build real connections with the sort of clientele you want."

"I'm working up to that point but it isn't as though invitations to exclusive events land in my mailbox every day." She shifted her weight and put her hand on one shapely hip.

He noticed them then. Patches of pink, shiny skin marring the creamy perfection of her fingers. This was what had made her instantly newsworthy when she'd come to Paris. The scarred, American heiress who wore her pain like a trophy and used her personal tragedy to her best advantage. Her sob story, the house fire that had left her burned, was half of her appeal to the media, and she made the most of it.

A quality he admired. Although, his first thought upon seeing that Ella Stanton's business loan was rolled in with the others he'd wanted to purchase had been to unload it as quickly as possible. He didn't have time to waste on a spoiled little rich girl playing at a career that suited her idea of over-the-top glamour.

After looking at her sales figures, he'd been forced to put that idea away, and talking to a couple of industry professionals and gaining insight on their opinion of Ella's talent had further altered his first impression. She wasn't playing; she was good at what she did.

She was working hard to advance her line, harder than he'd imagined she might be. But he knew he could take it further. Take her further.

The bottom line was profit; it was all that mattered. And he would wring every ounce of profit possible out of the Ella Stanton label.

"They do land in mine. And I know what to do when such opportunities for networking present themselves. I already have connections you can only dream of. I know you've read about my ability to crush companies if the need arises, but I can build them, too. In fact, I excel at it. The only question is which of my famed skills would you like to see employed here?"

There was a determined glint in her eyes, one that only served to add weight to the desire already settled in his gut.

"What exactly do you require of me?" she asked, speaking through her tightly gritted teeth.

"It's simple. When it comes to matters of business, you do as I say. To the letter."

"So all you want is total control then? Not too much

to ask." Her tone was even, her expression placid, but he could sense the barely controlled emotion that was all but radiating from her.

"What I want is to take your brand and make it a household name. To have every fashionista wanting the next big thing out of the Ella Stanton line. To have your clothing everywhere, from high-end boutiques to department stores. If I have to take control to see that happen, I will."

"What if I can buy out the loan?"

"You would rather try to keep going on your own than take this opportunity?"

"This is my business, not your moneymaking venture," she said, breathing hard, full breasts rising. He couldn't help but let his eyes linger there, to go further and admire the small indent of her waist, the round curve of her hip. A shame he didn't mix business with the pleasures of the flesh. It was too complicated, and when it came to women, he didn't do complicated.

"Do you think anyone would loan you money at this point, Ella? Your debt to income ratio is not the sort of thing a bank would want to see."

Color flooded her pale cheeks. "I know it's not what it could be but my plan is good and…"

"There are a lot of variables in your plan, from what I hear. And while it may be good in a general sense, it is not going to be guarantee enough for most banks as things stand. You've accumulated a lot more debt in the time since you took out this loan."

"Fashion shows are expensive. The last one I did cost me five figures, and I only earned a percentage back." Her voice cracked.

Ella felt like she was watching everything slide through her fingers. All the years of working toward something no one had believed she could achieve. She'd pushed herself so hard to make it this far. She'd done it on her own, without support from her family. The boutiques, the fashion line, they were hers. They were everything.

But now they were his. And unless she wanted to lose them altogether, she had to play his game. She'd known it would come down to that, from the second he'd shown her the paperwork, she'd known. She just hadn't wanted to accept it. But she had to now. There wasn't another choice.

Giving up her control, inviting someone else into her life, her business, was as close to a living nightmare as she could imagine. But losing everything went so far beyond a nightmare that she couldn't even think about it.

She sucked in a sharp breath and schooled her face into what she hoped was an expression of calm serenity. "I'm willing to work with you in whatever way I can to ensure our success."

A wry smile curved his wicked mouth. He wasn't fooled by her display of calm, and that made her angry. He could see through her, was amused by her. She curled her hands into fists and dug her fingernails into her palms.

"This isn't personal, Ella. This is about the bottom line, and I intend to see a substantial profit. If at any point it becomes clear that isn't going to happen, I will abandon the project."

Ella extended her hand and he grasped it. Lightning shot through her, unexpected, instant, as if she'd touched a naked wire. It mingled with the anger, the adrenaline that was already pounding through her and made her feel shaky, like her knees might give out at any moment.

She looked up and met his eyes, and saw heat. Attraction. He looked down at where their hands were joined, his large and dark, hers small and pale and marred. He ran his thumb over one of the scars that blazed a jagged path over the back of her hand.

The heat fled her, leaving in its place an icy shiver that made her feel cold inside. She pulled her hand from his grasp.

His gaze lingered on her. "It will be a pleasure doing business with you."

CHAPTER TWO

"HERE it is." Ella pushed open the door to her workshop and led the way in and Blaise followed. It had been a couple of days since their meeting in her boutique.

It had given him time to assess some of the other companies he now held loans for, and it had also given him the chance to decide that Ella's was the one he wanted to focus on. The more research he'd done, the more he'd become convinced that the moneymaking potential was there.

When he'd called this morning about seeing her studio she'd been irritated. Even now she was barely looking at him, blue eyes slanted the other way when she spoke to him. He found it highly amusing.

The workshop was spacious, with a flair that matched its owner. Each steel beam that ran the length of the ceiling was painted a different bright color, and the ceiling itself was done in black. It reminded him of how she dressed.

Today she was wearing black leggings and a long shirt that was belted at the waist. The top clung to her curves and he was hard-pressed to keep his eyes off her tight, rounded bottom as she walked ahead of him and to the back of the room.

"I keep all of my samples and patterns here." She

gestured to the back wall that was lined with rows of full racks, filled with brightly colored clothing.

"You have a large body of work."

She put her hands on her waist and blew out a breath. "I do. It's expensive work, though. I have a couple of investors, but the start-up alone was huge and shows are…well, they're more than I have at my disposal."

His eyes were drawn to her lips again, still painted that same bubblegum-pink. He couldn't help but wonder if she tasted like bubblegum. Or if she just tasted like a woman, sweet and earthy at the same time.

His body responded to the idea of that and he had to grit his teeth hard to fight the rising tide of attraction that was building inside of him.

"I'd like to take a closer look at some of the sales records for your boutique," he said, moving to stand in front of one of the racks, pretending to look at the clothing there.

He could hear her teeth click together. "All right." She definitely wasn't happy.

He turned to her and she looked away again. He cupped her chin gently and her blue eyes flew to his, wide and utterly shocked. It was the first time he'd seen her mask come down completely. It was fleeting.

"Did you need something?" she asked.

He ignored his body's emphatic *hell yes*. "Just those sales records. It's business, Ella. I need to know what I'm working with here."

"Sorry," she said curtly, stepping away from his touch. "I'm not accustomed to people rooting around in my things." She pulled a laptop out of the oversize bag she was carrying with her and set it on one of the worktables. She hit the power button then leaned forward, idly twisting the large, flower-shaped ring on her finger.

"I promise, it will be quick and painless."

She raised an eyebrow and gave him a sideways glance. "Is that what you say to your dates?"

The minute the words came out of her mouth, Ella knew she'd overdone it. There was a small, nearly imperceptible change in Blaise's expression, a curve to his full lips, a golden glint in his eyes. He moved to where she was standing at the table and leaned in, his eyes never leaving hers.

"My dates never need the reassurance," he said, his voice surprisingly soft, his face so close to hers that she could feel his breath fanning over the bare skin of her neck. She shivered slightly, hoped he didn't notice. "They know what they want, and they know I will give it to them."

Another biting retort clung to the tip of her tongue, but she held it back. Blaise had a well-established reputation, and he wasn't the only one.

She was known in the industry for being bold, even a little bit brash at times, but that was an act, a wall she put up to separate herself from the world. It was to keep the woman she was inside safe, protected by her facade. And in the context of small parties and backstage at shows, it worked well, helped her establish dominance.

But here and now, with Blaise, she was in over her head.

They were alone, and he was close enough that if she moved, just a little bit, her lips would touch his cheek. That thought made her throat go dry, made her stomach tighten almost painfully.

She turned her focus back to the computer and cleared her throat. She clicked on the folder that had all of her business stuff in it and turned the laptop so that it was facing Blaise.

He scrolled through a couple of spreadsheets, his expression never changing. He was like a solid piece of mahogany. Hard and unforgiving. Beautiful, too, but it didn't change the fact that a collision with him would be absolutely devastating.

"You do pretty well," he said, closing the laptop screen.

She let out a breath, one she didn't realize she'd been holding. But with Blaise, it always felt like she was waiting for the guillotine to drop. Waiting for him to decide none of this was worth it, to have him decide to call the loan in. Like it or not, their unwanted alliance was her best hope for a future for her clothing line, and that meant she needed to keep working with him, no matter how much it made her want to scream.

"Yes," she said. "I do. It's a small boutique, but it's in a prime location."

"And yet you have very little profit."

"I have almost no profit," she said dryly. "It's an expensive business. And now that the boutique has gotten busier, I've had to get employees."

No matter how successful she got in the industry, it required more of her. More time, more money, more manpower, and with every increase in income, there was an increase in cost. It made it nearly impossible for her to get ahead, and certainly impossible to make the kind of jump in status that Blaise seemed to want her to make.

"I like what I've seen here. I'd like to invest more." He named a sum that made her feel slightly ill.

He said it so casually, as though it meant nothing. Although, to a man with a billion dollars, or whatever it was he had these days, it likely was nothing. To a woman who ate instant noodle soup for dinner most nights, it definitely wasn't nothing.

She dealt in large amounts of money, but almost the moment they hit her bank account they were gone again, going to the next big thing. And this was more money than she'd ever thought to see in a lifetime.

"That's...a lot of money," she said.

"Yes, it is. But I don't believe in going halfway. I want this to be a success, and that means putting in the necessary investment to ensure that it is."

It was a slippery slope. It wasn't a loan: it was an investment, but this put her over her head in debt as far as she was concerned. It gave him more power. It pushed her out further.

But what choice was there? If she didn't take it she would keep on with her tortoise pace and Blaise would grow impatient. And that would be the end of everything.

None of this had mattered three days ago when Blaise Chevalier was just a name in the tabloids. But now he was the driving force behind the Ella Stanton label. Ironic that he even owned her name. It felt like he owned her. Allowing him to invest that much money would only tighten the chains that she felt closing around her wrists.

But it was all she could do, accept the fact the she was indebted to him until she could buy her freedom. At least at some point she would have the hope of paying him back, of buying him out. If she didn't go along with him she wouldn't have anything.

The bottom line, the amount earned, had never mattered as much to her as the level of success. She'd happily keep eating instant soup for the next ten years if it meant making herself a success at what she loved.

But that wasn't an option anymore, and what had only ever been a concern for her out of practicality had now become the primary focus.

"Then we both want the same thing," she said, even though it was a lie. He wanted money, and while she did want to make money, it was about more than that to her. It was about being something, accomplishing her goals. Becoming more than anyone around her had ever believed she would be.

A slow smile spread over his face and her heart thundered in response. She didn't know why. Except that when he smiled, it didn't look like an expression of happiness. It was more like watching a predator, satisfied in the knowledge that he was closing in on his prey.

She had a feeling that, in this scenario, she was very much the gazelle to his panther. She also knew that he was more than comfortable going in for the kill. A little blood on his hands wouldn't cause him to lose a moment of sleep. He was a man who accomplished his goals no matter who got in his way. Not a comforting thought.

"More or less," he said, slowly, his accent pronounced as he drew out the syllables, his voice enticing, despite the underlying danger. He didn't need to pounce on his prey, he could talk his prey into coming to him, and that made him even more deadly.

"Somehow I think as far as the method goes we might be more on the 'less' side than the 'more' side."

"Certainly possible." The deep, husky quality to his voice was shiver inducing. It made her stomach clench tight, made her entire body feel jittery, like she'd overindulged in espresso at one of the local cafés.

"Where are you from originally?" she asked, feeling stupid the minute the words left her mouth. Because it was his accent, and the strange curling sensation created in her stomach, that had prompted her to ask. And she really didn't want him to know that.

Didn't want him to think that anything about him interested her at all. Who knows what he might do with that bit of information.

"France, originally. My father is a very wealthy businessman, a native of France. But I spent a portion of my childhood in Malawi, with my mother."

"Why wasn't she in Paris?"

He shrugged. "My parents divorced. She wished to return to her homeland." He said it with as little interest, as little emotion, as he said everything. She couldn't help but wonder if it had really been so casual as he made it sound. To go from Paris to Malawi as a child couldn't possibly be a nonevent; neither could being separated from his father.

Although, she knew as well as anyone that sometimes cutting ties with family wasn't the worst thing in the world.

Still, it made her wonder about him. Made her feel a small sliver of sympathy for the boy he'd been. Why? He clearly didn't feel anything for her, and she wasn't asking for it.

They might have a tentative truce, but it was tenuous. She had his word, and his word alone that they would work on her business, rather than him simply wiping it out of existence by demanding money she didn't have.

Not a comforting thought considering his reputation. And that meant her mind had to stay on matters of business, and not the exotic flavor of his accent. Not on the boy he'd been, but the man he'd become.

"So, being that you're the mastermind," she said, breaking the silence, hoping to do something about the odd, thick tension that had settled between them, to get rid of that strange, tight feeling in her chest, "what are your plans?"

"I was thinking a Times Square billboard and a cover for *Look* magazine."

She coughed. "What?"

"I know the editor for the magazine. She said if I could get a look from you that would go well with a spring editorial that she would use it for an ad and the cover."

"But that's…that's huge exposure."

"*Oui*. I told you I was good."

"Very good." She felt like she'd been hit in the head, dazed and a little bit woozy. "It doesn't seem possible. She would do that, just because she knows you?"

"I had her look up your work online. She was impressed by you. It's hardly charity."

"But it's…"

"I told you I could turn your five-year plan into a six-month plan," he said, his tone laced with arrogance. "She might like to interview you, too. Do a designer profile."

It was the kind of exposure she both dreamed of and dreaded. The kind that would give her the success she knew she was capable of. The kind that would give her a lot of exposure, both personal and private.

She'd already dealt with it on a small scale. It was easy to just put up the wall, smile and laugh, turn for the picture to expose the scar on her neck. Give the people what they wanted. She didn't bother to hide the past, the marks it had left on her skin.

She also kept some of it to herself. She didn't want to flaunt the worst of it. She gave just enough, just enough that no one pressed for more. Not that there was anything left to be said that could hurt her. She'd heard every insult, every cutting remark. Some of it from the mouth of her own mother. She'd survived. She hadn't crumbled then, she wouldn't crumble now.

She was going to grasp the opportunity with both hands. Make the most of her unasked for association with Blaise. If the man could get her a billboard ad, a cover and an interview, she might grow to resent him less.

"That would be great, more than that, it would be amazing."

"I know you love publicity," he said, one side of his mouth curved up.

"I like the sales that come with it," she said, her voice flat.

Publicity, in a certain sense, she could take or leave.

"What would you pick for the shoot?"

Ella crossed the room, grateful for the distance between them. She didn't know what it was about him that made her feel tight and jittery inside.

His looks, his reputation, it all combined to make him a pretty potent mix. One she was afraid she didn't know how to handle. She worked with male models all the time, and their boyish quality didn't bother her at all. Sure, sometimes when she measured their finely toned physiques she got a mild thrill, but she was a woman after all, and they were men.

But it was nothing like the intense jumble of feeling she got when she just looked at Blaise. One part attraction mingled with a lot of nerves and anger.

And he was no boyish model. He was a man, a man who, if the tabloids were to be believed, knew exactly how to handle a woman in the bedroom.

She felt her cheeks getting hot and she turned her

face away from him, pretending to study some clothes on another rack. She bit her cheek again, harder this time. She had to focus, and not on how good Blaise's physique looked in his suit.

She had noticed of course. Everyone had a thing that attracted their attention and hers happened to be a well dressed man. But he wasn't her type; his suit was her type. That was the beginning and end of it.

She didn't have the time or the inclination to encourage some weird attraction to the man who had just performed a hostile takeover of her life. She didn't have the time or inclination to indulge in an attraction to anyone, but him most of all.

She could just imagine the look of abject horror on his face if she were to make a move on him. If he were to see the parts of her body that she kept carefully concealed. A man who dated a different, gorgeous woman every week wouldn't want to handle any damaged merchandise.

And she was that and then some.

"Blue, I think," she said, turning her focus back to the clothes. Back to her job. "This one." She pulled out a short blue dress with long ruched sleeves. "With the right boots this will be stunning."

She looked at him, waited for a flicker of…something. His expression remained neutral. "If you think it will work."

"Don't you want to weigh in?" she asked, both perturbed and relieved that he didn't seem to have an opinion on the matter.

"Why?"

"Because. Aren't we…isn't that why you're here?"

He came over to stand beside her, his eyes on the dress. When he reached out and took the thin fabric between his thumb and forefinger, rubbing it idly, it was like he was touching her hand again, running his finger over her scar. No one did that. Ever. Another reason she had no problem showing off the more superficial scars: it kept people from getting too close.

Not Blaise, apparently.

She touched the back of her hand, rubbed at it, trying to make the tingling sensation ease.

"I am not overly concerned with fashion. I leave these sorts of decisions to you."

"I have decision-making power?"

He turned to face her, the impact of his golden eyes hitting her like a physical force. "If I sat down at one of these sewing machines you would get nothing. I leave you to your expertise, you leave me to mine."

That was more than she'd expected from him. Far more. And yet, it didn't exactly inspire warm fuzzy feelings. He was right. If she walked, he had nothing. Nothing but sewing machines he didn't know how to use. An interesting realization. She'd underestimated her own power in the situation. And she would use it. She had to.

"So you're not expecting to dress my models for me?" she asked, keeping her voice stilted, cool.

"I never said I was."

"Your reputation goes before you," she said archly. "I thought I was dealing with a pirate. Someone who makes his living by preying on the bounty of others."

He chuckled, a rusty sound, as though he were un-accustomed to it. "All those stories you've read about me."

"They aren't true?" she asked, hoping, for some reason, that they might be lies. That he wasn't the callous, unfeeling man the media made him out to be.

"Every last one of them is true," he said, his eyes

never leaving hers. "*All* of them. My decisions are made for my own benefit. It is not charity that I allow you this measure of control, it is what's best for the company, and what's best for my wallet. That's the beginning and end of it."

It wasn't spoken like a threat. His voice was smooth, even as ever. Controlled. He was simply stating what was. But just like that, the glimmer of hope was replaced with a heavy weight that settled in her stomach, made her feel slightly sick.

"Right, well, I guess I'll take what I can." She hated that he made her feel so nervous, so unsure. She usually did better than this. She was accustomed to taking command of whatever room she was in, accustomed to having the control over conversation and interaction.

She didn't seem to have it in his presence. She couldn't even control her body's response to him. She wasn't even sure what to call the response. He scared her, which made her angry. He was attractive and when he looked at her the appraisal of his compelling gaze made her stomach twist. It was confusing. A mass of jumbled feelings she just didn't have time to sort through.

She breathed in deep, hoping to find the numbness that helped her get through life. That helped her get through uncomfortable moments. That helped her deal with people who wanted to hurt her.

She couldn't find it, couldn't shield herself from the things he was making her feel. He looked at her, looked at her as though he could see right through all the walls she'd spent the past eleven years building to partition herself off from the world. And she felt naked. Like he could see the worst of her scars, into her, past the damage on her skin.

"Do you have pictures of this dress?" he asked,

pulling her out of her thoughts, his focus on the business at hand helping rebuild some of her crumbling defenses.

"I take pictures of every piece. I have them in my portfolio."

"Excellent. Email it to me and I'll send it to Karen at *Look*."

"Yeah, I'll do that."

He turned to go then. Without even saying goodbye. It was like his mere move to exit should be sufficient. Standing in her own studio, he managed to make her feel like she was the one who had been dismissed.

She gritted her teeth against rising annoyance. Annoyance and something else that made her feel hot all over, made her face prickle.

She opened her laptop again and got ready to send the email to Blaise, using the address he'd so helpfully provided on the loan paperwork, those documents that gave him so much power.

So much power over her. She hated that. Hated him a little bit, too. This was meant to be her success, not his. The evidence of how far she'd come. Of all that she was capable of.

She attached the picture and left the body of the email blank. She didn't have anything to say to the man. She would work with him, do what she had to do to hold on to her business. And as soon as she could, she was paying him back and getting things back on track. Back on her terms.

She looked at the clock on her computer's task bar and swore mildly. She'd been invited to a Parisian socialite's birthday party and she needed to make an appearance. Blaise might not think it was effective marketing, but she thought differently.

He might own her business, but despite what she'd thought in her most dramatic moments, he didn't own her.

And she had a party to go to.

CHAPTER THREE

SHE was a pro at working a room, that was certain. Blaise tipped his drink to his lips but didn't take in any of the bubbly liquid. Alcohol and the buzz that came with it held little appeal to him. Losing control wasn't his idea of fun.

He watched as Ella talked to the small group of women that stood around her. She laughed, lifting up her foot slightly so they could get a better look at the electric-pink stilettos she was wearing.

The dress was sleeveless, showing off rough discolored patches of skin, the flesh on the upper portion of her left arm obscured completely by the marks. She seemed unconcerned, making grand, sweeping gestures as she talked.

He noticed that while no one looked at her with disdain, they did stand at a distance. He wondered if the scars were to blame. Ella didn't seem to care either way.

She was bubbly, confident. She was smiling, something he didn't know if he'd ever seen her do, not in a genuine way. But then, she didn't like him very much. Something he should be used to by now.

He set his drink on the bar and wove through the crowded club. Ella looked up from her friends and he saw her blue eyes widen, watched as her smile became forced.

"Mr. Chevalier, I wasn't expecting to see you here," she said, her manner smooth, but he could feel the strain it was taking for her to remain composed.

"I was invited, but wasn't sure if I could make it." This wasn't his usual scene. If he wanted to find quick and easy female company then he might bother with party attendance, otherwise, he had no reason to go to events like this.

Lately he hadn't even felt compelled to find a temporary lover. He found the games tiresome. Sex had been a catharsis after Marie had left, a way to try to wash away the memory, but now the endless stream of one-night stands had become boring. More than that, it filled him with a vague sense of disgust. Not anything new, but he found no reason to add to his sins.

Even now, one of the women in Ella's group was giving him a look that let him know all he had to do was ask and she would be his for the night. Knowing that a few months ago he wouldn't have hesitated to take her up on it made him feel a tinge of discomfort.

It shocked him. He couldn't remember the last time he'd cared whether or not his actions were moral. That ship had sailed a long time ago. Every last shred of honor he'd possessed had been stripped from him and he had simply embraced the man the world thought him to be. Because it was easier to be that man, easier to simply follow the path he'd started down than to retrace his steps back to the point where he'd gone wrong.

"But you did make it. Yay." She said it with about as much enthusiasm as a woman who'd just discovered she needed a root canal.

"Somehow, I knew you'd be happy to see me."

Her lip curled slightly, her smile morphing into a near sneer. She crossed her arms beneath her breasts, thrusting them into greater prominence, and a stab of lust assaulted him. It was unexpected in its intensity, especially after the clear invitation of the other woman had failed to arouse anything in him other than distaste.

"Well, I thought you felt these sorts of events were beneath you?"

"Not at all." The small group of women was quiet now, watching their interplay with avid curiosity. "Come with me."

"I'm fine here, thanks," she said archly.

"We need to talk."

The women looked from him to her, their eyes round with interest. One of them actually pulled out her cell phone and fired off a quick text, either to spread information or to try to garner some.

"Talk then," Ella said.

"Privately." He leaned in and took her hand in his. The action drew the attention of several more people in the crowded room, including guests that he guessed to be reporters.

He had noticed the last time he'd touched her hand, how shockingly smooth it had been, and the scar was even smoother, robbed of its texture by flames.

Her full pink lips parted slightly, her eyes round. She looked frozen, shocked by the touch. Didn't her lovers touch her like that? Or did they avoid the parts of her body that were less than perfect?

The women he'd been with had always been examples of universal beauty, the occasional botched plastic surgery aside. It was impossible to know what he would do if presented with her naked body. His liaisons didn't require that much thought. That was the plus side to one-night stands.

Of course, at the moment, the thought of Ella naked ruined his thought process anyway. It erased logic, left only that strong, elemental desire, desire that roared through his body with the force of a fire.

He tightened his hold on her and led her away from the group. Ella made sure he knew she was allowing it grudgingly, her body stiff as she walked behind him.

He drew her into an alcove away from the dance floor, the bass still throbbed, loud enough to make the walls vibrate. He leaned in, bracing his arm on the wall and Ella took a step away from him, her eyes widening a bit when her back came into contact with the wall.

She made him feel like an evil villain about to lure her onto the tracks. But then her mask came back down, her face serene, bight blue eyes glittering in challenge.

"So, what was it you needed?"

"A chance to talk. And we were drawing attention so I thought we might make the most of it."

"Okay, talk then."

"I must admit, I did not give you enough credit when we first met," he said.

Her expression registered surprise that she wasn't able to conceal. "What?"

"I didn't realize how much money there was to be made in fashion if everything is executed properly."

"Not an industry insider, huh?" she asked, dryly.

"Only if dating models counts."

She huffed out a laugh. "Unless your pillow talk consists of discussing the going rate for hand spun wool, no, it doesn't count."

"Then no, I'm not an industry insider."

She pressed her shoulders back against the wall, as if

she were trying to melt into the surface, her eyes focused somewhere past his shoulder. She tilted her head slightly and he could see that the pink scarring extended to the curve of her neck. It looked painful. Unhealed. And yet, from what he knew, it had to be.

It wasn't beautiful. It drew attention away from the creamy beauty of the skin around it. Uneven and discolored, it drew him, drew his focus. All of her did. He raised his hand and brushed his index finger lightly over the damaged skin. Surprisingly soft. Like the rest of her.

She pulled away from him, stepping back from the wall, mouth tight, the confidence she had displayed earlier, gone.

"Don't," she said, her voice sharp. She started to walk away.

"Don't?" He caught her hand and drew her back to him. She complied, but he imagined she only did so because every eye in the room was trained on them. His sex life was a constant fascination to the public, and any woman he was seen with was assumed to be a lover. He couldn't remember the last time it hadn't been true.

His muscles tightened at the thought of a night with Ella, his blood flowing hotter, faster. He responded to her on an elemental level, one that didn't seem concerned with the scars that marred her otherwise perfect flesh.

She leaned in so that he could hear her over the pulse of the music. "Don't touch me like you have the right to. You bought my business loan, you didn't buy me," she said finally, her voice low, trembling.

"I had not forgotten."

"So what was it then, morbid curiosity? It's called a burn scar, I got in a house fire. I would have thought you'd have read that somewhere by now. The *Courier* did a particularly nice article on the subject, if you're interested."

Ella's heart thundered heavily, her stomach churning. She hated that. Hated that the simple touch had done that to her. Every insecurity, every shortcoming felt like it had been thrown in her face, had been brought to glaring light.

She hated that the scars still made her feel that way. No matter how much she pretended to be fine with them, she still hated what she saw when she looked in the mirror. Hated the feel of them beneath her fingertips when she scrubbed herself in the shower.

No one ever…no one had ever touched them like that. The way he moved his thumb over the marks on her hand, the way he'd stroked her neck.

Only one man had ever put his hands on her scars, and that had only been with the intent of humiliating her, which he very thoroughly had.

Her mother and father had stopped touching her altogether after the fire. No loving embraces, no casual brushes of their hands. Nothing but cold distance as they wrapped themselves in their guilt. Even her pain became about them.

The soft, hot graze of Blaise's fingers had hit her with the force of an electric shock, shaken her out of her thoughts, tiny sparks of sensation continuing along her veins well after the initial contact. And then she had looked at him. At the smooth, mahogany perfection of his skin. She had been reminded then, of why she shouldn't let him touch her.

The stark realization had made her feel like she was drowning in shame and she didn't want him to see it. She didn't even want to acknowledge it to herself. Even now she wanted to break free of his arms and run out of the club. But she felt paralyzed, trapped. They were the focus of every guest in attendance and she knew there were reporters. She didn't want a reputation as the woman who ran out of a party like Cinderella fleeing the ball.

She was strong. She wasn't running.

"I suppose since you're in the habit of taking what doesn't belong to you, it didn't occur to you I might not be willing," she said, compelled to make him feel as exposed as she was. "Businesses. Women."

The change in his face wasn't drastic, but his eyes turned to golden ice, a muscle ticking in his jaw. "I only take what is not well guarded. Your business for example—if you weren't in so much debt, my power would be minimal."

"I see. So you're blaming me for this. Does that mean your brother is to blame for you stealing his fiancée? It was right before the wedding, right? You slept with her in their bed and then went public with her, touching and kissing her at every hot spot in town." The ice in his eyes melted, leaving a blazing fire, and every part of her body burned. She tilted her chin up. "You said every story written about you in the tabloids was true. Unarguably, that is what you're best known for."

He didn't flinch, the barb glancing off his granite defenses.

"Clearly you've done your research, but none of this is new information to me."

She had. She'd looked him up on the internet. And she'd allowed all manner of righteous indignation flood over her as she'd read about the betrayal of his brother because it allowed her to be angry at him. And being angry at him was so much safer than feeling anything else.

"I know my part in that incident very well," he said, his voice toneless. "I was very much involved, after all."

"A pirate in all manner of things," she said.

"I had never thought of it that way. But it's a nice way to romanticize it," he said, his voice a near whisper, his face so near hers now that it made her lips tingle.

"I'm not romanticizing. I find nothing appealing about a man with no honor."

He released his hold on her, strong, square hands curling into fists, the tendons becoming more prominent, showing the weight of the gesture and the intensity of the emotion behind it, even though his face remained smooth, unreadable.

"Honor. An interesting concept, one I've yet to bear witness to."

Join the club. She wasn't sure how much honor she'd ever seen in her life. As a teenager, stuck in a hospital room, it had made a nice fantasy. A knight in shining armor riding in on his steed. But she'd given up on that by the time she'd reached the end of high school.

And instead of a knight on his steed she got a buccaneer on his galleon intent on plundering twenty-five percent of her gold. Brilliant.

She looked up and his eyes locked with hers, she felt the heat again, inside this time, making her blood feel like warm honey in her veins, the ensuing languor making her reserve, her anger, begin to evaporate.

How did he do that? How did he make her melt inside with just a look?

Her lips suddenly felt dry and she darted her tongue out quickly, dampening them. She watched as his eyes followed the motion and she felt a yawning, aching sensation open up inside of her. She knew what it was. It was arousal, and she wasn't a stranger to it. She'd just never been in a man's arms while experiencing it. Had never had the object of her desire so close that she could place her hand on the hard wall of his chest if she chose to.

This wasn't a safe fantasy in the privacy of her bedroom. Not a dim, gauzy dream that sent vague sensations of pleasure rolling through her. This was a real, live, man. And he was looking at her lips with much more than just a passing interest.

No wonder his brother's fiancée hadn't said no. No wonder she had broken her commitment to be with him. He was temptation incarnate. His eyes, his chiseled physique, promised a woman pleasure beyond fantasy.

Oh, yes, what a fantasy. She flashed back to his finger skimming her scar. It wouldn't be a fantasy for him; it would be a waking nightmare. And she couldn't even fathom the thought of him seeing her, all of her. The idea was too horrifying to even contemplate.

And why was she thinking of it at all? It was like there was a war going on in her. Common sense versus basic instincts. It was a good thing she'd gained control over that basic part of herself a long time ago.

It suddenly felt unbearably hot, even though she was certain the temperature couldn't have actually changed. Or maybe it had. Maybe more people had filed into the small club and that was it. It couldn't really be him, his gaze, making her feel dizzy with heat.

He leaned in slightly and she didn't move, she stayed, rooted to the spot, keeping her eyes on his as he drew nearer to her. Her eyes tried to flutter closed and she caught them, wouldn't allow it.

She still didn't move away.

He stopped suddenly, his lips so near hers she could

feel the heat of them. "Don't worry. I don't need to possess honor to help make you a very rich woman. In fact, it helps that I don't."

The gauzy curtain of arousal that had been shrouding them lifted suddenly and broke her trance as effectively as a gust of icy wind.

"I'm ready to leave," she said, stepping away from him, finally.

"I'll stay," he said, golden gaze already wandering. He would probably stay and find some slim, sexy socialite to hook up with.

It made her feel ill, and it shouldn't make her feel anything at all.

"Good. Great. Have fun."

She turned and walked out of the club, embracing the chill of the night air as it hit her face. She needed it, needed a good dose of reality. What had happened in there wasn't real. It wasn't possible for a woman like her. And even if it were, she couldn't think of a single man she should want less.

It didn't change the fact that her heart was still pounding wildly and her body felt empty and unsatisfied. Didn't change the fact that when she closed her eyes it was his face that she saw.

CHAPTER FOUR

"It's headline news in the society pages," she said, still feeling numb with the shock of her discovery.

"The press has an unhealthy fascination with my sex life," Blaise responded, his voice still rich and enticing, even over the phone.

Ella stared down at the picture of the two of them, shrouded in near darkness in a secluded corner of the club, their lips nearly touching. Her stomach contracted and heat flooded her face. His body, so near to hers, so hot and dangerously tempting.

She shook her head and tried to banish the rogue thoughts. "I thought you said the press always printed the truth about you."

"Usually, if I'm with a woman, she's my lover. Or she will be by the time the night has ended."

That thought made her scalp prickle, made her breasts feel heavy. "Well, I'm not."

"No, but we were together. And they know I recently purchased your loan, a move that they presume was a bailout, a way for me to help out the current woman in my life."

"Shoddy reporting," she said tightly. "Someone needs to write a letter to the editor."

She sat down in front of her laptop and pulled up the

statistics for her website. It was something she did out of habit every day. She liked to know what brought people to her website, to get a window into the kind of people that viewed her work and to help get an idea of where she needed to buy advertising.

Her eyes widened when she saw the number of visitors she'd had, and they widened even more when she saw the keywords that had brought them to the site. Blaise Chevalier and Ella Stanton lovers. Blaise Chevalier Ella Stanton girlfriend. Blaise Chevalier Ella Stanton engaged. The last one made her inhale the sip of tea she'd been taking. She coughed into the phone.

"Are you all right?" he asked.

"I…I have about four times the normal amount of traffic to my website and…almost everyone was searching for information about the two of us." She looked back down at the article in the paper. "I…wow."

"That is the kind of press you need."

"And I got it at the kind of event you said was beneath me," she said, feeling the need to point it out because his superior tone grated.

"It helped that you were keeping the proper company."

That rendered her speechless for a full three seconds. "Your ego really is staggering," she managed to say.

"I fail to see how acknowledging my appeal to the media is evidence of my ego."

"Hmm."

"You disagree?"

She couldn't deny that she never would have gotten such a prominent feature in the society pages if it weren't for him. She couldn't deny that Blaise's aristocratic heritage, his reputation for being completely ruthless and his status as a first rate womanizer, and the fact that she was with him, were probably the key elements to the fact that there was any interest in her attendance at the party. But she didn't have to like it. And she could still think he had a big ego. Because he did. Any man who could callously walk off with his brother's intended bride and then, after the damage had been done, abandon her as well, was hardly a man of humility.

Or integrity.

But darn if he didn't get things done. His mere presence had created a mini media whirlwind. One that could only be good for her. And it hadn't even taken valuable advertising dollars to make it happen.

"I'll concede the point," she said, idly tracing the image of the two of them in the paper. Her eyes went straight to the biggest scar on her arm. Of course they'd taken the photo from her left side, her arm exposed by the sleeveless dress she'd been wearing last night. It was easy enough to feign confidence when she wasn't forced to look at the reality of her body.

She tossed the paper down on her table. "Without you, I never would have ended up in such a prominent paper, with such a large photo. The exposure was obviously worth it."

"Careful, my ego is growing."

"Ha-ha," she said, standing from her place at the table and walking over to the fridge, rooting around for a moment before closing the door, empty-handed. "I don't want to waste your time so I'll talk to you…when I talk to you."

She felt awkward suddenly. She'd called his mobile number, which he'd given to her. But for some reason it seemed personal. It seemed…it was awkward, which was why she *felt* awkward. That much she was sure of.

Of course, it wouldn't feel that way if she only felt

hostility for him, but try as she might, that spiraling, stomach tightening, heart pounding attraction just kept squishing down the resentment.

"This is business. I hardly consider it a waste of my time."

"Wow. That was almost a compliment."

"I've told you, Ella. None of this has been personal. I am not out to get you. I'm out to make a profit, and frankly, it only benefits you that I am."

"Yeah," she said, padding across the kitchen and moving to her living room window. She had a great view of the neighboring building's brick wall. "I get that. Because you make money, I make money, everyone's happy. But this is more than that to me."

"What more is there to business?"

Ella blinked. "Passion. A dream. The thrill of success, the feeling of accomplishment. There's a lot more to it." There was for her at least. Sometimes she felt like she was her fashion career. Like if it crashed and burned there would be nothing left of her. She'd poured everything into it. Time, money, hope.

If she failed…she just couldn't fail. It was everything.

"Ah, but unlike you, Ella, I *am* in it for the money. If something isn't profitable, I cut it loose. I do not waste my time."

"And I'm not wasting your time, so I suppose I'm meant to feel flattered?"

"Why would you?"

Oh, right. It wasn't personal. "Good question."

"I've had an email from Karen Carson, the editor of *Look*."

"Oh." She was excited to hear that, but a little bit

annoyed since she wanted clients to work with her, not her all-powerful, unwanted benefactor. "And?"

"She liked the photographs."

"Great, does she want the look for the ad?" Her heart was pounding a little bit harder, and this time at least it was over something concerning work and not Blaise's butter-smooth voice.

"Non."

"Oh…I…that's okay, it was a good try." And now all she could do was obsess about what she'd done wrong, worry about why her look hadn't been good enough. Why she hadn't been good enough.

Melodramatic much, Ella?

But that was the hazard of being so wrapped up in something. It felt personal when it shouldn't. It made her feel like she'd just been dumped. Which had never happened to her before, but she was guessing that was what it would feel like.

"She wants you to create something else."

"What?"

"The blue dress wasn't right, but she said she liked your…how did she put it?" He paused for a moment and she assumed he was skimming the email. "Aesthetic."

"Well, great. What does she want? I can do anything she needs me to do." She felt a little bit like an overexcited puppy and she had a feeling she might sound like one, too, but she didn't care right then.

"I'll forward you the message. She wants something more formal, something in that same color scheme. Something only for *Look.*"

The resentment she felt for Blaise was pushed down a little bit further. There were some definite advantages to this enforced, uneven partnership. Exposure like the article in the paper, and like this ad campaign, didn't just drop into a person's lap. At least they hadn't dropped into hers before.

Under normal circumstances she would have had to build a web of connections and climb the threads to get to the top, dealing with all the sticky hazards along the way. But she'd just skipped all of that, the boost from Blaise's connections propelling her much further ahead of where she should be.

"Thank you," she said, her throat suddenly, horrifyingly tight. She didn't want to do something stupid like crying. She didn't want to show him so much vulnerability.

"You have a strange habit of acting like a prickly little…hedgehog and then thanking me for something."

"A hedgehog?"

"Yes, that," he said, his voice matter-of-fact and full of certainty.

"Well, you have a strange habit of being a jackass and then turning around and making something pretty amazing happen, so I think it's a cause-and-effect kind of thing."

"A jackass?"

"Yes," she returned, "that."

"I've been called worse."

She knew he had. She'd seen it in black and white, in the tabloids, on the online gossip sites.

"So have I," she said, looking down at her hands, grateful he was just a disembodied voice on the phone and not actually here to fix those all-too-knowing golden eyes on her.

"I've forwarded Karen's email to you. You have about a week to get the dress made. They'll handle the styling."

"Great." Thank God they were off the personal topics and back onto business.

"I'll be by later in the week to check in on your progress."

"Great," she said again. Her body didn't get the memo that she was decidedly unenthusiastic about meeting up with him again and it immediately dosed her with a nice shot of adrenaline.

"Good luck, Ella."

"Only the weak need luck and magic," she said, repeating to him what he'd told her that first day. Reminding herself what sort of man he was so that her body would calm down a little bit and stop getting so darn excited every time he said something with that knee-weakening, stomach-tightening voice of his. "I don't need luck. I make fabulous clothes."

"Make sure that you do. Because if not, the ad could backfire on you in a major way, and I won't continue to support a dying business."

Her stomach tightened for an entirely different reason now. Annoyance and a prickle of unease spread through her. He was right—this was huge, and blowing it would cause far-reaching damage.

But doing it well would be the key to her success.

"I will," she said as she hung up the phone.

She would. She would make the best dress she was capable of, because everything was riding on this right now. And failing simply wasn't an option.

He was giving Ella special attention, or rather, he was giving her business special attention. He recognized it, and yet, he didn't feel compelled to change anything.

Blaise watched as Ella knelt down in front of the mannequin. She was fitting a pale blue gown to it, adding and removing pins, tugging fabric and humming absently.

He was struck again by how different her studio was than her neat, slick looking boutique. It wasn't a paired down black and white scheme with the occasional punch of color. It looked like there had been a color explosion in the converted warehouse. There were boards covered in swatches of fabric hung on the walls, bolts of fabric stacked into piles on the floor, on tables. A rack of bright threads, buttons and ribbons was at the center of the room. It was neat but chaotic in its choice of color and style.

A study in organized eccentricity. Like Ella.

She stood, tugging on the straps of the gown. Even now she matched the space she worked in. Tight dark jeans with bright pink stitching, the fabric clinging tightly to the perfect curve of her lush little backside, a black clinging top, a shocking magenta flower loosely pinning her wild blond hair into a low bun. Her look seemed casual, thrown together, and yet he had a feeling she worked for that effect.

There was no question that, as much as Ella might come across as some carefree, party-prone socialite, she wasn't that at all. Everything, even the chaos, was controlled and purposeful. That was something he understood. Control. Because without it, there was no limit to the depths a man might sink when he threw it all away.

Control was everything.

"That looks nice," he said, the compliment flowing from him with surprising ease. He didn't usually feel the need to give people that sort of assurance. But with her, he did. Perhaps it was the same, indefinable thing that had made him come here when a phone call would have sufficed as a means of assessing her progress.

Her shoulders bunched tight and she turned around to face him, blue eyes wide, finely arched eyebrows moved halfway up her forehead.

"Couldn't you, like…knock?" she asked, hand on her chest, bright pink fingernails glowing against the black background of her top. "You scared me."

"Perhaps you could try locking the door?"

"Is that your apology?" she asked, one hand on her hip now, her weight thrown onto one foot, causing her curves to become more exaggerated. Full breasts, small waist, absolute perfection. Perhaps her appeal was not indefinable. Perhaps it simply boiled down to her luscious figure, her enticing pink lips, and the fact they when he closed his eyes at night it was her image that left him hard and aching.

"How are things going?"

She narrowed her eyes. "Good. I thought you were just going to call or something."

"I decided to stop by and see how things were going. I like to have a personal hand in some of my larger investments." And the fact that her killer curves had played into the visit was something he was intent on ignoring. This was business. He kept his life compartmentalized, everything in its place. All the better to make sure he had a firm grasp on things.

Ella stepped slightly behind the dress form, her heart still thundering from Blaise's unannounced entry. He'd just startled her, that was all. But her body seemed to be having an awfully prolonged reaction to it. And it only got worse as he began to walk toward her, all fluid grace and hard, masculine lines. A compelling combination.

The deep charcoal suit he was wearing conformed

to his physique like a dream, the color the perfect foil for his rich skin tone. His shoulders and chest seemed impossibly broad. She had to add shoulder pads to suits for most of the male models she worked with and didn't get an effect half as dynamic.

It was easy for her to acknowledge interest and appreciation for his suit. That was her comfort zone. It was quite another to confess, even to herself, that she was more interested in what was beneath the suit.

"So, what do you think?" she asked, not because she really wanted to know, but because she was desperate to distract herself from the heavy tension that had settled in her stomach.

"It is…different."

"It's not made out of Lycra or covered in sequins, so I understand it might seem a bit out of the ordinary for you."

"A commentary on the women I date?"

"Um…yeah."

"Thank you for that, but I think the press has the commentary covered."

And he didn't care. She could hear it in his dismissive tone. Why did she care so much? Not about what the press said about him, but what they said about her. About the way her arms looked in a picture in the paper.

She just cared. She wished she didn't.

She cleared her throat. "Anyway, it's a mix of flow and structure, a little bit of Grecian inspired draping and the pleating on the bodice is to help give the model a good silhouette, and to add a more complex design element."

"If you say so."

He moved closer and she receded behind the dress form a little bit more. She didn't know where her bold confidence went. She was pretty certain she'd left it in the club a few nights ago. Darn him for being able to shake her like that.

It was one thing to play at a little bit of flirtation when she was certain a man would do nothing about it. Although when they saw the marks on her skin, they didn't want to go there. She was confident in the ability to use those physical imperfections as a shield.

But Blaise had touched them. He had looked right at them, not in horror. And he hadn't looked away and pretended not to see what was so very obvious.

He put his hands out, gripped the hips of the form and turned it slightly, his hands masculine and dark against the frothy, feminine fabric.

"I don't see any of that, I confess," he said softly, his eyes locked with hers. "But I can easily imagine a woman wearing it. The way these lines would conform to the curve of her waist." He ran his index finger lightly over the pleating she'd hand stitched into the bodice. "And these lines here—" he let his finger drift over the gown, up to where the pleating was done more loosely, with wider strips of fabric "—to make the woman's curves look even more dramatic."

She sucked in a breath as his finger skated over where the breast would be. She felt her own breasts grow heavy in response, felt her nipples get tight, as though he were touching her.

And all the while one large hand was resting on the hip of the form. She could almost feel the weight of his hand on her body, anchoring her to the ground so she didn't float away.

He moved his hand down, grazing every fabricated curve on the dress form before gripping the filmy fabric of the skirt.

She could feel it. What it would be like to be in that gown. To have his touch firm and sure, over every swell and hollow of her body, to have him take a handful of the skirt of her dress. Maybe he would push it up next. The fabric would glide over her body with ease, cool and light, while his touch would be hot and heavy in the absolute best way.

The air suddenly seemed thick and it was a struggle to draw breath. A struggle to stop her knees from buckling.

He dropped the handful of fabric he'd been holding, his eyes still locked with hers. The faint whisper of the chiffon, mingled with her strangled breathing and her heart pounding in her ears was the only sound in the room.

Her lips tingled, her body ached. He hadn't put his hands on her, and yet she felt branded. She felt as though something major, something completely altering, had happened, when all he had done was touch fabric draped over a dress form.

"I certainly wouldn't mind if my date showed up wearing this," he said, stepping back, appraising the gown casually as though…as though all he'd ever been doing was looking at the dress.

Because of course, that was what he'd been doing. That was all he'd been doing in his own mind. It was her mind, her sex-starved body that had made it into more than it was. She'd had too many fantasies. Fantasies where men looked past the imperfections of her body and desired *her,* the woman beneath the scars.

Although, even in those fantasies, she never saw herself as damaged. When she thought of being in a man's bed, his hands moving over her back, her mind saw smooth, flawless skin. Her mind made her beautiful, a match for her dream lover. It was a lie.

And so was the moment she had just conjured up in her mind.

"Great. I think Karen will like it, don't you?"

"As I said, fashion is not my thing. As a man I can say I would be drawn to the ad."

"Well," she said, her throat still tight, "hopefully women like it, too, since they're the majority of *Look*'s readership."

"I'm sure they will."

"Thanks." Now she just wanted him to leave, so she could forget what she'd just felt. So she could think of him as the pirate and not as the man who had set her body on fire with just a look, not as another thing she wanted that was forever out of reach.

There was no reason for her to want him. In this instance, the scars were offering protection. She shouldn't want any part of the man he was. Of a man who thought so little of betraying those he was supposed to love.

Focus on that. Not his muscles.

"I did have one other thing I wanted to speak to you about," he said.

Great. "What?"

"I want to take you to the sort of event that will actually be of practical use to you. I'd like for you to go to the Heart's Ball with me tonight. Perhaps we can give the media something more to talk about."

CHAPTER FIVE

THE Heart's Ball was one of the biggest charity events in France, if not the world. Tickets were amazingly expensive, and that was only for entry. After that, there was dinner, which would cost around three hundred Euros a plate.

All of it went to fund the Heart association, aiding people with heart problems, helping them pay for medications and surgeries. It also helped the rich and famous rub elbows with each other and give some good PR.

And there was no way Ella could ever afford the cost of the event.

"Are you footing the bill?"

"Naturally. I always pay for my dates."

"I want to buy my own dinner," she said, wincing as she thought of giving up that amount of money. "It's a good cause, and I'd like to support it myself, too."

She realized, a little too late, that she'd just agreed to go with him. But how could she not? He was right, and the web traffic didn't lie. If being seen in a club at a minor celebrity's birthday bash was enough to make the news, then this would do even more for her.

She would love to refuse, would love to say "I don't need you or your publicity." But the simple fact was, she did. She needed it badly. Spending time with him was, ironically, the key to getting rid of him faster. The key to getting the money she needed, to getting her control back.

If that meant spending a few hours in his company, she would do it.

Her body prickled with heat, a treacherous physical excitement building in her as she thought of him holding her close to him, like a man would a date. It was highly charged, adult version of the guilt she used to feel as a child when she was about to do something she knew she shouldn't do.

But she wasn't going to do anything. She wasn't. But she couldn't stop the little pulses of adrenaline from spiking in her, couldn't hold back the slow arousal that was building along with it.

"I will buy your dinner. You can make a donation in the amount you see fit," he said, that voice hard and uncompromising. As much as she wanted to argue with him, her bank balance made it seem like a very stupid idea.

"All right, that sounds…no it doesn't sound fair, it still sounds lopsided."

"A man should always pay for his date. What manner of idiot do you usually associate with?"

"Oh my gosh, did you really just give me a lesson in chivalry?" she asked, bristling because no one had taken her on a date since high school. And that had ended… badly. Badly enough that she still didn't like to think about it.

"You seemed to need it."

"Not from a man like you." And she regretted that the moment it left her mouth. Because while Blaise could be hard to deal with, he'd never insulted her. And she'd lashed out at him deliberately more than once now, using his past against him. If he'd done the same to her, she would have been devastated. Although, she doubted it was possible to devastate Blaise.

He didn't react to the barb, not hugely. Nothing beyond the slight tightening of his jaw. "Not from a pirate like me?"

"I didn't…" She sucked in a breath, regret and oxygen filling her. "Forget it."

"No, you did, and you're right. I'm not exactly the sort of person who should give advice on how to live in civilized society, and I don't claim to be. But one thing I do is take care of the woman I'm with, whether I'm with her for a night or for a long-term relationship."

She could well imagine that he did take care of them, in a physical way at least. His smooth voice spoke of all kinds of pleasures, pleasures she couldn't begin to imagine with her nonexistent experience. But physical was about all he would be good for. Nurturing didn't really seem to be his thing. His track record was poor to say the least when it came to caring for those he supposedly loved.

She looked at him, at his chiseled face, so hard it seemed to be carved from stone, and she felt an instant stab of guilt for the thought. And why, she didn't know. Only that she, of all people, should know better than to take people at face value.

Blaise seemed almost too comfortable with his role of villain at times. So much so that it made her wonder now what was beneath it.

Nothing. Don't go there.

She wasn't going to allow herself to pretend that he wasn't exactly who he appeared to be, just because she wanted him to be. It was something she'd done with her parents for years until the stark realization had hit her that they would never, ever love her more than they loved themselves. Would never be able to look beyond their own grief to see hers.

People didn't change just because she wished they would.

"What time is the ball?"

"Eight," he said, brushing his fingers lightly over the front of the gown that was still pinned to the dress form, making another little zip of sensation shoot through her.

She clenched her teeth. "Then you'd better go so that I have time to get ready."

"It's meant to be a costume party, by the way."

The excitement was back, building, growing, along with a little bit of anger, anger that he so easily called a response from her body. And desire to get revenge. To make him burn with the same physical discomfort that she burned with every time she looked at him.

To make him ache for her, as she did for him.

"Now, a costume, I can do."

Everything at the old châteaux where the Heart's Ball was held was draped in glittering lights and gemstones. Swathes of fabric hung from the ceiling, and ornate, hand folded paper hearts had been placed on every surface.

All of it spoke of an excess that had long ago stopped impressing Blaise. Although it certainly had at first. All of it, the wealth, the grandeur had been a source of fascination to him when he'd returned to Paris at the age of sixteen. When he'd left, he'd been a boy, but after eight years away he had been ushered into a whole different world. His family, his father and brother, had wealth and influence he could scarcely remember, and they had welcomed him into it.

But in the fourteen years since, he had begun to see the grime on the highly polished facades of the elite that frequented these events. He had been tarnished with it himself, had gone on to spread it to others.

No, the setting held no appeal to him. But Ella, her body wrapped in crimson lace that barely covered her long, shapely legs, lace that gave hints of the pale skin beneath without revealing too much of her lovely curves, she had the power to turn his head. Interesting since it had been at least three years since a woman had possessed the ability to do anything but arouse him in a generic, physical sense.

Passing sexual interest was common enough, but the burning ache of desire that Ella had ignited in his gut was another.

"What are you supposed to be?" he asked, taking her hand, a hand that was covered by fingerless, lace gloves, and leading her down into the ballroom.

Her lips, cherry-red tonight, curved into a smile. A gold mask covered part of her face, making her eyes look even brighter, more mysterious. "I'm temptation."

Yes, she was. And three years ago, he would have set out to give into that temptation with single-minded focus. He would have allowed his desire for her, for the satisfaction of his flesh, to overrule his mind.

But he wasn't that man now. He had seen where that led. He believed in control now, in the denial of that part of himself when it was appropriate to deny it.

"What are you supposed to be?" she asked, giving his black suit a critical once-over.

He leaned in, the scent of her, light, feminine, teasing him, making his stomach tighten with arousal. "I'm a man who does not like to wear costumes."

He was rewarded with a laugh, a genuine laugh that

seemed to bubble up from somewhere deep inside of her. "Well, I sincerely doubt anyone will challenge you over it."

"I would imagine not."

His reputation was too cemented, too ingrained in the minds of everyone here for them to give him so much as a wrong look. But he knew they all thought unflattering things. He was the boy who was all but raised by wolves in the wilds of Africa, as far as they were concerned. The man whose father had welcomed him back, sent him to the best college, attempted to make a success of him. The man who had taken his father's efforts and made a mockery of them by betraying his brother, the older man's much beloved heir.

Fine, he used the public's perception to his advantage. It left him free to do what he liked, it gave him very little competition, mostly because the general public imagined there was no low he would not stoop to.

And he thought they might be right. Was there any lower for him to go? He seriously doubted it.

"That isn't fair you know," Ella said, giving him a smile, a genuine one. A strange thing for him to be on the receiving end of.

"Why is that?"

"I dressed up."

"Yes, you did." The lace looked so delicate, it would be easy to tear from her body, exposing her to him, one gossamer strip at a time. He could kiss the color off of those cherry lips. He would maybe leave the mask, though. It made for a very naughty image. Ella, naked except for the golden mask.

He would know it was her, though. There was no question. Even in his fantasy of her, the marks on her arms were there, the discolored skin on her neck. The scars that signified her as Ella, and not just some face-less woman.

Ella felt as though Blaise was looking straight through her gown, which was, admittedly a little on the daring side. It was thin, but with enough fabric to obscure the bits of her body that needed obscuring, either for public decency or for her own vanity.

At the moment, she was very grateful for the mask. It felt like a little something extra to hide behind.

"When do we get to sit down to this extravagant dinner?" she asked, eager to get a table between them, something to help divide his focus, because at the moment it was very much on her mind and it made her feel totally edgy.

It had been empowering, putting on the short, shocking dress in her bedroom, imagining getting back at him for the episode in her studio. She'd wanted to put him off his footing a little bit, like he'd been doing to her.

But no, he was still making her feel uncomfortable when she should be feeling confident. Clothes usually did that for her. That was just one reason fashion had become such a passion for her. By taking control over her looks, by playing to her own strengths, she could completely change people's perception of her. And that appealed to her immensely.

It was failing her now, though. She felt like she'd overplayed her hand a little bit. Because when he'd come to pick her up and his golden eyes had slid over her, appraising her, he'd looked like he might devour her.

And what would she do with a man like him if he did decide to do that? What would he do with her?

Probably run screaming from the room once he got the dress off, horrified that he had nearly sullied himself by making love to someone who was so disfigured.

Maybe her scars weren't that bad, but they were all she saw when she looked at her body. And she hadn't been tempted to try to find out what someone else might think, not since her disastrous prom date with the boy whose aim had been to get her top off so he could see just how ugly she was.

Not since the only comfort her mother had been able to offer was a softly murmured, "you used to be so beautiful."

No, she hadn't felt like trying since then. And if she ever did…it would have to be with someone she really knew. Someone who really cared for her. Not someone who was just lusting after the facade she managed to show the world.

"Later, I think they want to give everyone a chance to schmooze first."

"Is that the technical term?"

"I believe so, but I have never been one for it."

She could believe that. Blaise didn't seem to care what anyone thought about him. In fact, he seemed to go out of his way to be aloof half the time.

It was opposite to the way she handled social situations. If she feigned confidence, if she was the one to instigate conversation, then she had the control. It was the same idea as the daring lace dress. Show confidence no one can question, and they'll be too afraid to issue a challenge. Combine that with her scars, something that seemed to set most people on edge, unsure of whether to look or look away, and she usually had the upper hand in social situations.

Unfortunately it didn't seem to work that way with Blaise. Of course, she expected there was very little in the world that could possibly intimidate him. He seemed outside of laws and, therefore, exempt from the usual reactions she got from those around her.

In fact, he met her challenges head-on. Even touching her. She could feel it still, if she thought back to that night at the club. His fingers drifting over her skin, skin that had been untouched by anyone other than herself. Who else would want to touch it?

She still didn't know why *he* had.

"Well, maybe we can schmooze with each other," she said, regretting it as soon as it left her lips. "What I mean is…we can talk business."

"Right," he said, snagging two glasses of champagne from a passing waiter's tray. He handed one to her and she took it, grateful to have something to hold on to. Grateful to have something to distract her.

The way he was looking at her, the way he had been looking at her, from the moment he'd seen her tonight, set her teeth on edge and made her body feel restless, aching. Needing. Wanting.

But there were just too many reasons why not to give in to all the demands of her body. And even if she did try to give in, there were two people involved. Facing the rejection, the look of disgust on his face, should he decide he didn't want her once he unwrapped the entire package…she didn't want that. She could survive it, but there were a lot of things she could survive that she didn't necessarily want to experience.

"Right," she said lightly, taking a sip of her champagne. She didn't want it going to her head. She didn't really have a legendary alcohol tolerance and Blaise already made her feel dizzy without adding anything else into the mix.

"How is the gown for *Look* coming along?" he asked,

those wicked golden eyes appraising her, making her insides feel like warm liquid honey. He was reminding her of just what had happened earlier in the day, that gown acting as the centerpiece to her mini downfall.

She had wanted, so badly, to lean in and touch him. To press her lips to his. To make him feel what she was feeling.

She blinked. "Great. About the same as it was when you left this afternoon. Karen had already seen a sketch and was pleased with it, so I'm feeling confident. As confident as I can feel over something so huge."

He shrugged and she noticed he hadn't taken a drink of his champagne. "Every step you take is another step. I treat every business deal with equal importance. That way, I never let anything slip."

"Hmm." She tapped on the side of the glass. "And it keeps you from getting too nervous over something big, I guess."

"I don't get nervous."

"Never?"

"No. I make a decision and I act on it. I don't do nerves. I don't do regret."

The tone of the conversation shifted, Blaise's voice getting darker, his tone hard. She wondered if that was true. If he moved through life with no regrets. If he had truly stolen the love of his brother's life, then discarded her, with no regret at all.

Part of her, the physical part, that was looking into his eyes, that could see the uncompromising set of his jaw, the tightly clenched fist at his side, that part could believe it. But something inside her didn't. Couldn't. She didn't know why because she was pretty sure that in this case, she should believe her eyes and not her silly, fantasy-prone heart.

"That must be…freeing."

She could see how it would be. She regretted a lot of things. Things she'd never had the ability to control. Things she'd never made a decision on, but that simply were. Things that twined around her, ensnared her like a rabbit in a trap.

"Interesting choice of words," he said, managing to sound coolly disinterested even now.

"Not really. It must be nice to have so much confidence in everything you do."

"You never seem short on confidence, Ella," he said, his tongue all but caressing her name, his accent making it sound exotic in a way she'd never noticed before.

He leaned in slightly and she lowered her eyes, desperate to avoid his gaze. But she just ended up fixated on his fingers as they stroked the stem of the champagne flute, the motion making her think of his hands on her skin, stroking, caressing.

"Although," he said, "sometimes your cheeks get a little bit pink. Like now."

She took a step back. "It's hot in here."

"Would you like to step outside for a moment?"

She nodded, heading for the balcony, away from him. Except that he was coming with her, which totally defeated the purpose.

"I'm fine," she said, welcoming the cool night air, waiting for it to penetrate her heated flesh, to knock a little bit of common sense into her, and some of the clouding arousal out of her.

"It is bad form for a man to leave his date."

"Again with the chivalry?"

"I am just ever conscious of my glowing reputation."
His voice was tinged with sarcasm, and a hint of bitter-
ness that made her think that, although he really wanted
her to believe he lived with no regrets, it probably wasn't
completely true.

"Or at least of what the caption might read beneath
our names in tomorrow's news," she said, hoping to
lighten the mood a little bit.

She leaned back against the balcony's railing and
looked at the glowing white lights, woven between the
overhanging lattice that was also draped with grape-
vines. If she could only focus on that instead of the man
standing near her, she might be okay.

"It will be interesting to see, that's for certain."

"Especially since we've now disappeared onto the
very private balcony for what can only be described as
a tête-à-tête."

He laughed, the sound shocking in the quiet night,
shocking because it had been so silent, and because it had
come from Blaise. "You should work for the media."

"I don't have the stomach for it," she said.

Strains of music from the ballroom filtered through
the open doors and Ella closed her eyes, enjoying the
soft, subtle sounds.

"You like it?" he asked.

"Yes. Club music isn't really my thing, to be honest."

"But promotional opportunities are?"

"I've met a lot of people, a lot of clients, by spending
time at the right nightclubs. But I very much consider it
business and not pleasure."

He reached out and took the glass of champagne from
her hand, setting it, along with his, on the stone railing
behind her. He touched her hand, a soft touch that sent
heat feathering through her, gentle and pleasant.

Then he took her hand in his and drew her to him, slowly. And her feet moved to him, her body leaning in, far before her brain had a chance to catch up.

He looped his arm around her waist, pulled her to him.

She knew the expression on her face was quite possibly one of dumb shock, but actually having him touch her, being in full contact with his body, was a shock to her senses. Her breasts were pressed against his very hard chest, the delicious pressure working to ease some of the ache that had been building in her.

"I thought you deserved a chance to dance, as you enjoy the music so much," he said, his breath hot against her ear as he whispered the words. She shivered, goose bumps breaking out over her arms.

"Oh," she said, heart hammering so hard she was certain he must be able to feel it against his chest.

She didn't know why she didn't pull away. Why she didn't say no.

No, she did know. It was because it felt good. And she had felt so much pain in her life it just felt…it felt so foreign and amazing to just let herself feel good.

To revel in the warm weight of his hand on her lower back, the feeling of his other large hand enveloping her much smaller one. Swaying with him, moving in one accord with him instead of just fighting him. Instead of fighting herself.

"Temptation," he whispered, his cheek against the curve if her neck, his words a whispered enticement. "Such a fitting choice of costume."

He released her hand then, placing his on the curve of her hip, moving it to the indent of her waist, stopping just beneath the swell of her breast. She had imagined his touch earlier, felt the slide of his fingers as he'd moved it over the gown she was making.

But that had been fantasy, just like it always was for her. But this was real. His hands on her body, the thin red lace the only barrier between his flesh and hers.

The rhythm of the music seemed to fade and they made their own, his movements so slow and sensual, seductive on a level she could have never imagined. And when he moved nearer to her, she felt that he was as aroused as she was, the hard length of him pressed against her a proof that couldn't be denied.

He moved his head, hot breath tracing a line from just beneath her ear, over her scar and to her shoulder. His lips never touched her skin, only hovered there, making her body tighten with need, making her want to pull him to her so she could feel the press of his mouth on her.

She wanted it. So much. So much that it scared her, made her feel hollow and nervous and like she might fold in on herself if she couldn't have more of him, more of his touch. His hands on her skin, without the dress in the way, his lips, not just the impression of them.

She swayed slightly in his arms, her breasts brushing against his chest, sensation pouring through her, drowning her senses in desire. Being in his arms, just held by him, so close, was beyond anything she'd ever experienced, anything she'd ever imagined.

She tilted her head to the side, exposing more of her neck to him. Warm breath continued to tease her, the tip of his nose skating lightly over the delicate skin.

He pulled away, looked at her, then gently tilted her head the other way, repeating the action with the other side of her neck. She stiffened when she could no longer feel his heat, when she lost the sense of the slow glide of his touch. She put her hand to the back of his head, felt that he was still there, touching her. But she couldn't feel it.

There could be pain or pleasure, heat or chill, and she wouldn't know. The scar that distorted her skin was an outward sign of the damage that lay beneath. Nerves lost that would never be recovered, feeling she could never regain.

She released her hold on him, jerked back, stumbling slightly. "I'm sorry," she said, helpless to say anything else. It wasn't really an apology, not to him. She was just sorry. More of those regrets. "We should see about that dinner, maybe?"

His was an unreadable mask, his body stiff. "Are you hungry?"

She was sick. Her stomach felt as though it had been filled with leaden weight, her entire body shaking. "It's late. And anyway, it really should be spectacular, gold dusted chocolate cake or something." He still didn't move, didn't speak. "Thanks for the dance," she said, because there really was no way to ignore it. All she could do was try to make light of it. Try to pretend her whole world hadn't just been shaken. It seemed like she'd been trying to pretend that ever since Blaise had stormed into her life.

He nodded and offered her his hand. She clenched her teeth, tight, trying to hold back frustrated tears. She couldn't touch him now. If she did, she might crumble.

But she wasn't weak. She never let anyone see her cry, and she wasn't going to start now.

"I think I can manage to find my way back into the ballroom," she said stiffly, keeping her hands at her sides.

A small smile curved one side of his mouth. "Of course."

At least now there would be a physical barrier between them, a table, and maybe some wealthy society people to create a buffer.

Although, now it all just felt like too little too late.

CHAPTER SIX

Chevalier Romance Heats Up!

The press had done their job admirably. They hadn't missed the chance to snap photos of a very rare event: Blaise Chevalier with the same woman twice.

Not for the first time, he felt a small stab of disgust over the interest the media had with the salacious details of his life. Over the fact that there were so many salacious details. He was not a saint, not by any stretch of the imagination, and the press didn't have to tweak too many truths in order to write stories about him.

But he used his reputation to his advantage, no reason not to. He made money. It was what he knew how to do. It allowed him to set up foundations in Malawi in his mother's memory. Support causes that had meant so much to her.

The money that he made, the success he had achieved in business, was the one thing that kept his father from writing him off entirely. Not that he truly sought out redemption, not from him. Their relationship was strained at the best of times, his father still harboring anger at Blaise's eight-year-old self for choosing to leave with the woman who had betrayed him.

Then there was Luc. That Luc had offered forgiveness

so freely for what had happened with Marie was still something that didn't settle well with Blaise.

It would have been better, in so many ways, if his brother had demanded a pound of flesh for the betrayal, if he had worked to extract pain and revenge. But he had not. And there were times when Blaise felt there was still penance to be paid.

Although, that implied that he was seeking absolution. He was not. Such a thing was beyond men like him. He accepted it. Owned it. Used it, as he did all things.

Just as he knew he and Ella could use the press to their advantage in the building of her business.

Ella. Temptation.

She was, much more than he had envisioned. Women, in his mind, were women. Sex was sex. Looking at it any other way had drastic consequences. But Ella, her smell, the feel of her skin, the temptation of those full, brightly painted lips of hers, turned him on faster than any woman in his memory.

Even Marie. And the control he had allowed Marie to exert over him had been nothing short of shameful.

He knew the man he was when he allowed emotion to lead. Knew what he was capable of when he let his desires take charge, when he abandoned decency in the pursuit of his own satisfaction. He had no intention of ever being that man again. Which was why his control was his own now, why he never allowed it to be shaken.

He put the paper down on his desk, allowing his gaze to linger on the photograph of Ella and himself out on the balcony. His face was tilted down, close to the curve of her neck.

Her head was tilted back, her face in profile. Red lips parted, eyes closed, long lashes fanning over her high cheekbones. She was a beautiful woman, no question about it. But there were many beautiful women. Women who didn't come with so many strings attached. Women who didn't test the edges of his tightly leashed control.

His mobile phone rang, the name *Karen Carson* flashing on the screen. "Chevalier."

"Hello, Blaise," she said, her voice tinged with a little bit of flirtation. Invitation.

He'd met Karen on a few occasions, but their meetings had been strictly platonic. From the sound of things, she wouldn't mind a change.

He entertained the thought for a full second, toying with the idea of using her to take his mind off Ella. He'd done it before. There had been countless women after Marie, each one used to try to wash away the impression the only woman he'd ever cared for had left on his body.

The thought of doing that now filled him with disgust, and he wasn't sure why.

"Is there something wrong with the sketches Ella sent you?"

"No, I quite liked them," she said, taking a cue from him, her voice hardening into a more businesslike tone, the flirtatiousness evaporating.

"Then all will go ahead as planned? The cover and the ad?"

"A cover now, too," she said, not sounding terribly surprised.

"Ella is very talented. I want to see that talent rewarded."

Karen cleared her throat. "Ah, yes, well as I've seen in the news recently there is speculation that you know a great deal about her talents."

The note of jealousy in her voice made him tighten

his jaw out of annoyance. Ella had talent; he believed that now with a decent level of conviction. He wasn't about to have this opportunity dangled before her, only to have her lose it because of a woman mourning the loss of a night of sex that he'd never had any intention of having with her.

"I am only a man," he said, "but I am also a businessman. If I didn't think this would be a good move, for your magazine and for her, I wouldn't suggest it."

Karen cleared her throat. "Actually I was so impressed with the sketches I was thinking of including some more Ella Stanton pieces in a spread we're doing. There will be several designers represented. It will be very good exposure for her. We're thinking a beach shoot in formalwear. Very dramatic."

"Dramatic indeed. Have you scouted locations?"

"We were thinking Hawaii."

"Boring," he said. "Overdone."

"And you have a better idea?"

"Naturally."

"Do you have enough staff to cover a week away?"

Ella jumped slightly, gripping the edge of the counter to keep from losing balance on her three inch heels. "You really like the whole unannounced entrance thing, don't you?"

"I couldn't reach you by phone."

"The boutique has a phone," Ella said, jabbing the old-fashioned rotary phone with her finger.

"Charming. Does it work?"

She narrowed her eyes, hoping to capitalize on the annoyance that was currently flooding her. It was easier than dealing with the wild galloping of her heart.

"Of course it works. But you wouldn't know, because you decided just walking in her would be better."

"It's a public place, isn't that what most people do?" he asked.

She clenched her teeth. "Yeah. Anyway, why didn't you call my cell?"

"I did. It went straight to your voice mail."

"Oh." She crouched down behind the counter and fished around in her magenta leather bag, finding her phone buried at the bottom. Either she'd switched it off or the battery had died. Great. Very professional. "Sorry," she said, putting it on the counter.

She flashed back to what he'd said when he'd first walked in, registering the words for the first time rather than just that voice that sent her heart rate into overdrive.

"You asked if I could go away for a week?"

"Karen would like you to consult on the photo shoot. She wants your gown for the cover and the billboard ad."

Excitement tugged at her stomach, excitement that had nothing to do with Blaise for once, and everything to do with the achievement. This was so big. It was a key, to bigger and better. To worldwide exposure. To runway shows she couldn't even afford to buy tickets to now.

"She wants me to consult? She wants my opinion?"

"She'd also like for you to bring some additional looks, for a spread they're doing in the same issue that has your cover. She wants formal gowns. On the beach. I've been told this is very high fashion."

"It is," she said. "I think...I think I'm going to hyperventilate."

"*Non, belle,* don't do that," he said, brushing his knuckles lightly over her cheek.

She pulled back, decided not to acknowledge the touch, or the lightning fast pulse of pleasure it sent streaking through her. "Yeah, um…so when do we leave?"

"Tomorrow. Can you have everything covered here?"

"I should be able to work that out. Yes, I will work it out." She started mentally rebuilding the boutique schedule in her mind. Because she was going to grab this opportunity with both hands, no question.

"Good."

"Are you…I mean, how am I getting there?"

A slow, sexy smile curved his lips. "We will be taking my private jet."

Her eyebrows shot up. "That's extravagant."

"Not really, it's a small jet."

"And you're coming, too?"

"Of course." He said it as though it should have been a foregone conclusion, and it really should have been. Still, a slug of surprise hit her stomach, followed by a tight curling of pleasure, similar to the kind that had assaulted her the night she'd gotten to be his date for the ball.

"We're doing the shoot in Malawi," he said. "It's a very tropical setting, the lake has water so clear you can see all of the fish swimming beneath the surface. It is the most beautiful place in the world."

There was a distance to his voice, a strange detachment. He said it was beautiful, and she believed him, but she also thought there was sadness there. Sad memories maybe. She thought again of him as a boy, leaving Paris, leaving everything he knew, his father, to go to a new country. A very different country. What had it been like? Had he been scared?

She couldn't imagine it now. Even in his well-cut suit he looked like a battle-hardened warrior. He didn't look like a man who had any concept of fear, or failure or any of the things that mere mortals seemed to struggle with.

He was a man apart. She envied him for it. She also wished she could come into his world, just a little bit. And it was so not the right thing to wish for.

"I'm…I'm looking forward to seeing it." She almost said she was looking forward to sharing it with him. But that was the wrong thing to say, the wrong way to look at it. Blaise wasn't going to share with her.

Those words, those thoughts, didn't even have a place in her mind. Neither did the ache that was spreading from physical body parts and beginning to lodge itself in her heart. She didn't know what to do with it. There was nothing to do with it, and yet she couldn't seem to shake it off.

But then, she was currently enduring steady doses of Blaise exposure, so that wasn't helping.

"Bring clothing suited to very warm weather," he said, the heat in those honey-gold eyes only reinforcing the demand.

"Okay," she said.

If only there was a way to cool down the warmth that Blaise brought with him whenever he was within ten feet of her. If only there was a way to forget how he'd touched her the night of the Heart's Ball.

But she couldn't. She was marked by him. And she knew that some marks didn't fade easily. And some of them lasted forever.

"So, I'll see you tomorrow then?" she asked, anxious to get him out and away from her so she could have a little time to herself before she embarked on a week filled with his presence.

"Where would you like to be picked up?"

"My studio…it's below my apartment so that will be easiest." And then he wouldn't have to come up to her apartment and be in her space. Because if that happened, the impression of him would officially be embedded in every aspect of her life, and she just didn't want that. Not even a little bit.

"Then I will see you tomorrow morning."

"Yeah, see you then."

Sleep wasn't going to come easy tonight.

Ella could definitely get used to luxury travel. None of the nonexistent legroom or intimate acquaintance with the shoulder of the person next to you. Not to mention the fabulous perk of being able to bypass airport security.

Blaise's "small jet" had turned out to be a heavenly travel experience. Complete with silken leather seats that reclined all the way and champagne with strawberries.

The only drawback had been the fact that, even though he sat on the opposite side of the cabin, it was a lot of Blaise in an enclosed space. It gave her ample chance to really get tuned into his smell, his movements, short noises he made in his throat when he was thinking. And all of it made her stomach twist just a little more each time.

It was an effort to keep from squirming in her seat after an hour of travel. Being alone with him. Being so near him. The futility of the desire, that was the worst part. She was burning with need for him, and she knew that she could never arouse the same kind of desire in him. He was masculine perfection, the kind of man who could entice women to trade in their favorite pair of shoes in exchange for a night of pleasure in his arms. There was no way he would ever want her.

When they landed on the island of Likoma, she practically kissed the ground, so thankful to be out in the open, to detox from her Blaise overload. To try to regain some of her sanity.

A sleek black car, heavy and old-fashioned, but in pristine condition, met them at the tiny airport and she was whisked from the burning heat back into an air-conditioned environment.

Ella settled in the backseat, her relief at exiting the plane dipping sharply when the door to the car closed and she found herself getting cozy with Blaise again.

"It is beautiful here," she said, looking at the shoreline of the vibrant lake as they passed, the green trees and the shocking blue of the lake blending together.

It wasn't what Ella thought of when she pictured a lake. Waves crashed against the sandy shore, children splashing in the vibrant, crystal-clear water.

She smiled, watching them laugh as the cold water washed over them. She wondered if she'd ever been so happy as a child. Maybe she had been before the fire, but she couldn't remember. Her family had had everything. Money, status in the community. It hadn't protected them. And it hadn't offered her any comfort when she'd needed it most.

"In my opinion, the natural beauty you find here is unmatched. But there is much to be done as far as helping the people with the quality of life. It is better now," he said. "I've been working to improve the infrastructure, the roadways, trying to make things more accessible, that's been another challenge. Health care facilities, hospitals, clean water systems. And yet, there is always more." He sounded tired. She didn't think she'd ever heard him sound tired.

"You…you've done all of that?"

He shrugged, clearly uncomfortable with the subject. "I have done small things. It is what anyone would do."

Except it wasn't. It wasn't something anyone would do, and it wasn't small. And the media had never once said anything about Blaise's charitable efforts. The only time his heritage was mentioned was in a derogatory fashion.

In Paris, he seemed rootless, a rogue. A man who didn't care what others thought. He took action swiftly, decisively, without care for how it affected others so long as the bottom line was well-served.

Not here. Here were his roots. Here was his responsibility. Something he cared for more than money. People that meant more to him than a bottom line. He'd said that business was not the place for charity, but apparently he believed it had a place.

He'd also said he didn't believe in honor. But his honor was here, too.

"We'll be doing the shoot here," he said, gesturing to the shoreline.

"It will be dramatic. I love the idea of formalwear in this environment." She was happy to be back to the safety of business. She tried to keep her mind there by imagining what hairstyle she would have the stylist do with each gown, what sort of makeup.

The distraction was short-lived. Because Blaise was still right next to her, close and so very male and tempting.

She shivered slightly, even though it was hotter than blazes outside and the air conditioner only served to take the edge off. She wasn't cold. She was hot inside. Burning up. Consumed with an internal fire that she had never allowed herself to confront before.

It wasn't that she had spent eleven years void of sexual desires. She had simply channeled them into fantasies about movie stars, heroes in books. Men she would never meet, or, better still, weren't real. Men who couldn't reject her.

It was more than a fear of rejection, though. It was the bone-deep fear that her mother was right. That things would be easier if she had died in the fire instead of living with the damage, confronting her mother with the damage, left behind.

But things wouldn't be better. She could do anything she wanted, fulfill her dreams. She was in the most beautiful place she'd ever seen, with the most beautiful man she'd ever seen, on the edge of the biggest break of her career.

And even though she would never truly have the man, it wouldn't stop her from enjoying the fantasy.

She looked at Blaise again, watched him as he stared out the window at the passing landscape, square jaw enhanced by the angle of his head, rich mocha skin begging for the touch of her lips, a taste from her tongue.

Somehow, being so near to him, the memory of his fingertips gliding over her skin, made all of those fantasies that had always been sufficient seem pale.

"Where will we be staying?" she asked.

"Another thing I have been working toward, bringing more tourism into the area. There is no shortage of attractions, but accommodations for wealthier guests have been limited."

"And you've taken care of that, too?"

"Yes," he said simply, turning his focus to his smartphone.

She had a feeling that she was getting close to seeing the man that Blaise truly was. And she could tell that he didn't want her to see it.

CHAPTER SEVEN

ELLA hadn't anticipated the absolute decadence of the resort. She should have. It was Blaise's, and he didn't do anything in half measures.

It was hidden from the harsh sun beneath a thick canopy of trees. Built from stone and covered in vines, it looked as though it had grown up from the impossibly beautiful landscape. It was cool, calm and completely inviting.

"We will be staying in my personal villa," he said.

"We?" she said, her face starting to burn, and not from the heat.

"I have given it some thought. The Heart's Ball created a huge media stir. The press loved the more…intimate photos they were able to capture of us."

"And?"

"And I would like to give them some more fodder."

"The press won't be here will they?"

"Ella, there will be models, stylists, writers, photographers and a photo shoot director. I think someone might mention something. Especially as I'm certain there were photos taken of us boarding the plane in Paris this morning."

"Oh…you think there were?"

"If the press wasn't taking a day off. I made no effort

to be discreet. The press are weaving a romantic fantasy around our association and it is attracting a lot of attention to your clothing line. And this time, whoever wrote the article about the two of us mentioned you were wearing one of your own designs. He also named you best dressed of the night."

"I...I saw that." Seeing the pictures that had been taken of the two of them, some when they had been on the balcony, so close, desire so clear in her eyes it had horrified her. But the article had been wonderful, and the next day she'd had two women into the boutique asking about the red lace dress.

So he was right. The media was paying attention, and as a result, so was the public. But the idea of shacking up with him for a week was a little bit disconcerting.

"I'll have my own room, right?"

"It's a big villa. You won't have to see me if you don't want to."

That wasn't what concerned her. It was that she did want to see him. It was that being near him made him long for things that she had no business longing for. Not now, not with him.

The Town car bypassed the main building and drove them down toward the shore. The villa was situated at the very edge of the covering of trees, the front door nearly resting on the white sand beach, the crystalline water lapping at the shore a mere fifty yards away.

It was made of stone, just like the main building, the roof fashioned out of woven grass. It was like a private island fantasy. Like the two of them had been shipwrecked. Shipwrecked with the pirate—there was a nice one to save for later when she was in her bed. Alone. Aching. Longing.

She turned her thoughts off that particularly depressing track and back onto the scenery.

The slight rusticity of the environment dissolved the moment they walked into the villa. High ceilings, that were plastered, proved the woven grass was for show. White stone floors and French Provincial style furnishings gave it a look of timeless, expensive elegance. The curved, sweeping staircase that led to the second floor made it feel palatial. And Ella felt like a princess for a second. A feeling that was so foreign she thought she might be dreaming.

And then there was Blaise, and the feelings he created in her. Now that was complicated. There was the desire, desire that had been there since day one, and then there was the growing tenderness. A well had opened up behind the walls surrounding her heart and seemed to be expanding.

Coming here with him had changed the way she saw him. It had opened up another side of the enigma to her. This wasn't simply a moneymaking venture for him. She knew that. Sensed it. This brought in tourism, and with it, tourism dollars. It created jobs.

It forced her to look at him in a new light, though she didn't want to. Even when she thought he was nothing more than a cold, ruthless man who would stop at nothing to get what was his, a man who would think nothing of betraying his brother, even then it had been hard enough to stop herself from weaving fantasies around him.

Add this unexpected glimpse into his humanity and she felt like she might be in serious trouble.

"I will ask that dinner is served soon," he said.

"I can find something in the kitchen." The idea of spending a quiet, intimate evening filled her with excitement, which gave way to mild panic. She should feel that way about him, about spending time with him.

"Ella, must you always be so stubborn?"

"I think so."

"For once, don't. Tonight, just enjoy yourself."

"Okay," she said.

Her heart thundered hard in her chest. Because nothing scared her more at the moment than the thought of giving in to what she really wanted and truly enjoying herself. Because, if she did, she not only faced the possibility of rejection, but of Blaise seeing how weak she truly was.

The scene was set for seduction, and never had there been a woman who looked more ready to be seduced. Blaise could only stare at Ella when she came down the stairs and met him in the open living area of the villa.

Ella, with her loosely contained blond curls accented by a shockingly pink flower. Ella, with lipstick and a daring dress to match. The neckline was too high for his taste, denying him the sight of her luscious breasts. But the fabric was fitted, clinging lovingly to every dip and curve of her body. And the hemline was brief, showing more of her mile long legs than should be legal.

It was the first time he'd seen her in simple, flat sandals, and he imagined the only reason she'd abandoned her daring high heels was out of deference to the sand.

He hadn't realized quite how petite she was. She seemed softer, more delicate this way. And it made his stomach tighten with urgency. He wanted to shield her, from what he didn't know. And to make her his.

And that he understood very well. He knew just what sort of possession he sought. The most basic, elemental sort. Her soft body beneath his as he found satisfaction within her, as he gave her pleasure, took his own pleasure.

The strength, the immediacy of it, was beyond anything he had felt in so long. He couldn't remember if he'd ever felt that way. He had shut down so much of himself after Marie because he had seen what happened when he gave his emotion free rein. It was an ugly thing.

"Dinner was set out for us on the terrace."

"Oh, nice," she said, but she didn't really sound like she thought it was nice.

"Were you expecting different?"

"I just thought...maybe a restaurant."

"Are you afraid to be alone with me?"

She blinked rapidly, pale gold lashes sweeping up and down with the motion. "I...why would I be?"

He took her hand in his, and she let him, curling soft slender fingers around his. "I don't know," he said, tracing the back of her hand with his thumb.

"Well, I'm not. I just thought we would go out. I'm overdressed."

"You look perfect. As always."

He watched as her pretty pink lips wobbled, only for a moment, before she set them into a firm line again. Her blue eyes looked brighter than usual, suspiciously so. "I will accept the compliment," she said, her voice thick.

How could such a simple compliment touch her so? Careless words, words he meant, but not words he had spent time thinking over. Nothing he hadn't said to another woman, only to be treated to a petulant pout until he expanded on the sentiment.

Not Ella. The simple, pure reaction was totally honest. He wasn't sure what to do with it. It made him want to say more. It made him want to offer to take her out, somewhere where he wouldn't be tempted to seduce the woman with the steel exterior, but possibly fragile interior.

But no, Ella wasn't fragile. She was tough. She was confident. He had simply caught her in an emotional moment, and heaven knew women had plenty of those.

He continued holding her hand, and she continued to hold his, as he led her up the stairs and through double French doors out to the sweeping terrace. White lanterns hung from the sheltering roof, introducing a soft glow to the warm, purple evening.

The view of the lake was stunning, the table setting was stunning. But neither thing touched the beauty of his companion.

Ella sat down before Blaise could do something else sweet. Like pulling her chair back for her or something. She already felt like a wreck.

You look perfect. As always.

She had never been perfect. Not before the fire. Certainly not after. And he had stripped her bare of every last piece of armor with the compliment. Because it was a tease of the one thing she'd always dreamed of. The longing she would never even say out loud, not even in an empty room.

To have someone accept her as she was. Love her as she was.

It was such an impossible fantasy. She didn't love *herself* as she was, how could anyone else? Least of all a man like Blaise. A man of such physical perfection, who dated women possessing the same physical perfection. It was impossible.

But her mind had taken that little thread and

immediately begun weaving a web with it. One of pretty words and happy endings. Lies.

She picked up the wineglass that was, thankfully, already full and touched it to her lips, taking a small sip. Anything to distract herself.

"This looks great," she said, placing her glass back on the table. It was inane conversation, but the grilled fish and bright, fresh vegetables did look great and at least it was a safe topic.

"Naturally."

"Because you only hire the best in the world?" she asked, arching one eyebrow.

"I had the best in the world come here and train some of the local people. Everyone that works here is from Malawi."

More of that tenderness spread through her. She could almost feel her heart melting.

"How old were you when you came here?" she asked. She shouldn't ask. She didn't need to know. And yet she wanted to know.

"I was eight. But I didn't live on the island. I lived on the mainland, just outside Mzuza. My mother worked at a bank there. We were not impoverished, as so many others here are."

"But why did your mother bring you here?" She'd wondered. She knew his brother had been raised in France with their father.

"It was part of the deal," he said, his voice rough. "If she left Europe, she could have me. Otherwise, she would never see either of us."

"Why…why would your father do that?"

He slid his fingers up and down the stem of his wineglass, a muscle in his jaw ticking. "I think he was hurt and he wanted to hurt her back. I also don't think he believed she would truly go. It is my understanding that she had an affair, although, I have never been angry at her for it. I think when they fell in love they were perhaps a bit idealistic. They were able to see past cultural differences, skin color difference, and then many others were not. And there was tension."

Blaise leaned back, releasing his hold on the glass. "They imagined that love would be enough. It was not. Of course, things have changed now. I don't believe there would be the same issues. I've certainly never had them, and I have dated all types of women. But at the time..."

"And you came with your mother," she said softly.

"I wanted to," he said, "I never regretted it."

"When you came back...did you hate your father for what he'd done? For...banishing you?"

He shrugged. "My father is a hard man. He demands perfection. Control in all areas of life. I don't regret that I wasn't raised with him. But I don't hate him, either. All of us act poorly at times when passion is involved," he said, his voice taking on a bitter tinge.

She wondered if he was thinking of himself now, if he regretted the affair with his brother's fiancée. She wouldn't ask, though. Not now. She didn't want to engage in an exchange of information.

"True," she said. Not that she would know.

Her life had been so void of passion. She had channeled it all into her work. Everything had gone into her work. But it hadn't felt as all-consuming lately, hadn't felt quite as essential. Which she imagined was good. Feeling so much about anything was dangerous, as Blaise had just pointed out.

It was strange, though, feeling like her focus was splintered. Since her senior year of high school she'd moved toward her goal of having a successful fashion career, and she'd done it single-mindedly. Nothing had distracted her. She'd gone to Paris, she'd studied business and fashion in college, she'd gotten low-level jobs, gotten loans, started her own boutique and clothing line.

Nothing had ever turned her head away from that. Until now.

Now she saw the beauty of the setting she was in, the food tasted more intense, flavors bursting on her tongue. Her skin felt sensitive, her entire body on edge. It was as though a part of herself that had been dormant had just woken up.

Her focus had broadened. Her desires had broadened.

Blaise was looking at her, the same glittering heat in his honey eyes that she'd seen at the Heart's Ball. Her heart started pounding harder, her palms growing damp, her stomach so tight it made it hard to draw breath.

She stood from her chair and walked over to the edge of the terrace, looking at the lake glittering in the pale moonlight. It was beautiful, a natural wonder. It made her feel empty. Because she suddenly realized she'd never truly enjoyed the beauty of her surroundings. She'd always lived with such manic desperation, to be better, to be more successful.

Then Blaise was standing beside her, his large masculine hand gripping the wrought-iron rail. Before meeting Blaise she'd never really stopped to admire the differences between a man's hand and a woman's hand. She had never stopped to appreciate the effect that difference had on her.

He lifted the hand she'd been so focused on, cupped her cheek.

She lifted her eyes, met his gaze. It was easier in the

dim light. He slid his hand down her neck, the undamaged side, and she shivered at the sensation. He leaned in, pressing his cheek against hers, his skin hot, roughened by stubble.

He pressed his lips to the hollow beneath her ear and a sharp groan escaped her lips. It was shocking. It was pleasure beyond anything she'd known before, that brief brush of his mouth on her tender flesh.

He kissed her again, this time on curve of her neck, the tip of his tongue teased the skin there. He raised his head, golden eyes searching hers.

She wanted to beg for him to kiss her lips, and yet she didn't want to alter his plan. She wanted to see what he would do next. Her heart was thundering in her ears, drowning out thought and reason, drowning out everything but the kind of desire she'd only ever dreamed about.

He kissed her again, his lips brushing the corner of her mouth this time. His hand cupped the back of her head, his fingers worked into her hair, gripping her, clinging to her as though he had to hold her to him. It thrilled her that she could affect a man like him. That he wanted her.

She felt her lips part of their own volition, her tongue sliding out to moisten them. He took it as an invitation, and she was glad, because she'd certainly meant it as one.

He didn't crash down on her like a wave. He dipped his head slowly, his lips hovering over hers, sending sparks of need raining through her. Her entire body begged for his touch, but her lips ached.

He rubbed his nose against hers, slowly, lightly, before closing the distance between them. He teased the seam of her lips with his tongue, but she was suddenly afraid to move. Afraid that if she did, she might wake herself up, that she might discover it was nothing more than a dream, and that she was alone in her apartment in Paris.

One hand still buried in her hair, he snaked the other arm around her waist, hand spread over her back, the heat breaking her from her fog. This wasn't a dream. Blaise was real. And he was kissing her.

She parted her lips for him then, gladly, enthusiastically. She shivered when his hot tongue slid against hers, exploring her mouth, tasting her, savoring her as though she were a delicacy.

She felt her hands unclench, lifted them so she could cling to his shoulders. If she didn't, she would simply melt into a puddle at his feet.

The boys she had kissed hadn't prepared her for a man like Blaise, couldn't possibly have prepared her for the tidal wave of desire that a simple kiss had sent crashing through her entire body.

He untangled his fingers from her hair, one hand anchored on her hip now, the other roaming over her curves, cupping her breast, his thumb sliding over her nipple until it ached, until she felt hollow and needy, ready and desiring to be filled by Blaise.

"I have to touch you," he whispered, abandoning her mouth, lowering his head to press a kiss to her cloth-covered breast.

His hand reached around to her zipper. "Ella," he said, his voice husky, thick with desire.

She shock of air that hit her skin, the slide of the zipper and the cold reality of her own name, brought her back to her senses, and with it, brought a rush of panic.

This had been a fantasy. She had been floating,

allowing herself to pretend. But her name, whispered on his lips, was like getting doused with a bucket of cold water.

She wasn't the sort of woman who made love with gorgeous men beneath a blanket of stars. She wasn't the sort of woman to inspire that sort of desire in a man, any man, but especially one like Blaise. She was just Ella. She was the woman with disfiguring scars. The virgin whose lack of experience proved just what an insecure, damaged person she was. If she were to sleep with Blaise, he would know that. He would see her worst, he would see her fears, her pain. How could she show him that? How could she ever show anyone? It was less about her skin, more about her. About the scars beneath her skin, the weakness.

"No," she said, releasing his shoulders, her hands flying behind her back to stop him from lowering the zipper further.

"No?" he asked.

"I can't. I can't. Oh, I'm so sorry, but I can't." Words came out in a jumbled rush, and she felt tears pooling in her eyes, ready to spill.

She was devastated. She was angry. She was scared. And she still wanted him more than she wanted her next breath. But she couldn't.

When he touched her, he was in charge, he commanded her body, he orchestrated the movements. And she had nothing to cling to. No facade of confidence, of being at ease with herself. She didn't want him to know, didn't want him to see into her, to see all her insecurity. All her fear.

She turned and went back into the house. And she cursed. She had run away. She was the worst kind of coward. And she was too afraid to be anything else.

CHAPTER EIGHT

"THE art director wants the blue boots." One of the gofers for the photo shoot was standing in front of Ella, the sand colored boots she'd selected for the china-blue gown dangling from her fingertips.

Ella gritted her teeth. It had been like this for most of the day. They had Ella give her opinion on accessories, makeup and hair. And then the director sent the model, or the shoes, or the belt back to be changed.

Ella reached behind her to the bag full of shoes and rifled for a pair of sky-blue velvet ankle boots. She handed them back to the gofer. "Here. I'm sure these will translate better in pictures."

Grudgingly she had to admit they probably would. They would make a brilliant foil for the white sand beach. She was just touchy because of Blaise. More specifically, because the imprint of Blaise's lips was branded on her skin, and her own cowardice, her own fear, was laughing quietly over its victory.

Fortunately Blaise had been absent for the entirety of the shoot so far. Ella moved from beneath the tents that had been set up on the shore to provide the crew with relief from the sun and went to stand near the photographer.

The wafer-thin model with pale blond hair and dark

eye makeup was most certainly working her look, contorting her body in a way that made her look like a sad, beautiful, broken doll.

A little shiver of excitement wound through Ella, momentarily chasing away her annoyance and regret. The model was Carolina, a very highly sought after editorial model, and to see the woman in her designs was like seeing her dreams truly come into fruition.

"She looks good." Blaise's voice penetrated her reverie and brought reality back in on her.

Ella didn't turn toward the sound of his voice. If she did…the flashbacks would ensure she ended up melted into a puddle. "She does."

"Going well?"

"Yes, we're almost done for the day. Tomorrow we're going to move to an inland location, have her pose in a waterfall."

"You are sure this magazine is meant to sell to women?"

Ella turned sharply this time. "It's not going to be a wet T-shirt contest. It's high fashion."

"My apologies." He sounded amused. She cursed him mentally twenty different ways.

"This isn't a men's magazine," she added, for good measure, knowing she sounded like a prude.

"Point taken."

The director called it a wrap and Ella started to wander back to the tents. Blaise followed.

"Haven't you got…somewhere to be?" she asked.

"No. I'm through with my business for the day."

"And what did that business include?" she asked, in spite of the fact that she should be trying to get rid of him, not continuing a conversation with him.

"Discussing the drilling of more wells in some of the

outlying villages. And getting more ambulances, mobile care units, something to help the people who live far out of the cities in a medical crisis."

Ella stared at him. "You carry a lot of weight on your shoulders." She heard herself say it, and realized how true it was at the same time.

Piercing eyes appraised her. "So do you, I think."

A crushing amount. "Not really." She shrugged, trying to remove the heavy feeling. It was impossible. "I wanted to thank you," she said, clinging to her water bottle like it was her life support, keeping her focus on the bright blue label, and away from Blaise.

"For?"

"Not for—" she felt her cheeks get hot "—I just wanted to thank you for this. All of this. I know that our working relationship has been...rocky. But I'm grateful for it now. This has helped." She still planned on paying him back as quickly as possible, but what he had done for her in such a short space of time simply wasn't something she could have accomplished on her own.

"It is business, Ella. Nothing more."

"But there's more to you than that," she said. She didn't know why she said it, why she wanted him to admit it.

"Not really."

"What you do here, in Malawi, that's not just business."

"Don't be fooled by a few charitable acts, Ella. A tax write-off is a tax write-off."

Her heart tightened. She didn't believe him for a moment, but watching his face get hard, seeing his walls come up around him, that hurt.

Her defenses seemed permanently crippled, and his remained as high as ever. Blaise was perfectly happy playing the bastard, even as it became abundantly clear there was more to him.

The way he had treated her last night was an example of that. He didn't plunder, or take. He had given to her. His lips had been both gentle and firm, demanding and generous. And when she had withdrawn, he had respected her.

It wasn't only his response that offered her the window into him. It was the fact that he was using the same methods she had used for the past eleven years. Don't let anyone in. Don't betray any emotion.

He was better at it than she was, though. Something she'd envied at first. Something she wasn't sure she envied anymore. She felt like she had one foot behind her own emotional walls, one foot testing out the other side.

She was afraid. Last night she'd been too afraid, and today she'd tried to resurrect her defenses to no avail.

She looked at Blaise, at his profile, his body held so strong and masculine, his posture so straight a military officer would be envious. He was a sinner, it was widely known. But he also built hospitals and dug wells.

And he had shown her things about herself, unlocked things in her she hadn't imagined were in there.

She had stepped into the fashion industry, a woman with scars, a woman who had been tormented by the fashionable girls in high school. And she had done it without fear, without hesitation, because it was her dream.

Last night, she'd wanted a man. She'd wanted Blaise, so much she trembled with it. And she had let her fear have dominion over her. She had seized control in her professional life, had set out to achieve her goals with single-minded focus. Why should any other area of her life be different?

It was time for her to stop being afraid.

He had been up half the night, his body aching, unfulfilled. He wanted Ella. His mind had been plagued by images of her, naked, her nipples, pink and tight, begging for his touch, her lips, soft and moist on his body.

All day he had pictured her blue eyes filled with desire for him, with none of the abject terror he'd seen flash in their depths when she'd pulled away from him on the terrace.

He would kiss her neck again. The curve of it, where it was smooth and creamy, the other side, where it was not. Not for the first time he thought it strange that his fantasies did not make her body unblemished. In his mind, he pictured every scar that he'd seen before. Because that was her. It was Ella. And his body, for whatever reason, desired only Ella.

And every mark that signified who she was.

His body tightened, hardened as he thought of her. She was so soft. He could imagine, very easily, the feeling of every soft inch of her pressed against his body.

He had left the photo shoot before Ella today, but he knew she would have returned by now. He closed his laptop and leaned back in the office chair. He'd thought to check on some of his investments to distract himself, but stocks weren't doing anything for him. Not tonight. Not when he knew Ella was somewhere in the house, downstairs probably.

This desire, this need, had a strength that bothered him.

Obsession. He remembered it well. Had vowed never to allow himself to give in to it again. That driving need to have something, someone, regardless of the cost. It was a weakness. A lack of control. That he was weak at his core was something he preferred to forget.

But Ella reminded him. Because Ella stirred up a kind of specific longing in him he hadn't felt since Marie. Then he had called it love. Had imagined that it made a sufficient excuse to act purely for himself.

"Love conquers all," he said bitterly. Love was a lie. An excuse.

He knew better now. What he felt for Ella was lust, nothing more. Strong lust, the sort of lust that promised untold pleasures, but only lust. Human desire at its most basic.

He had enough experience with that to recognize it. But with Ella, it was so much stronger. She made everything feel stronger. He needed to find his cool passivity again, his detachment.

The temptation she presented seemed too great to combat. All the more reason for him to do so. He had to maintain control. He had seen what happened when he didn't.

He would not indulge himself, would not give in to the need that was pounding through him, making his hands shake with the effort it took to keep from going downstairs and finding her, kissing her, making love to her. He had to prove he could stay distant. He couldn't afford anything else, anything more.

He needed to find another woman when he got back to France. That thought cooled his ardor faster than any cold shower ever could.

The breeze blowing in from the lake was cool; it blew across Ella's heated skin and made goose bumps raise up on her arms. She had not seen Blaise for most of the day.

She wasn't avoiding him now because she was scared of him, she was avoiding him because she hadn't decided what she wanted yet, and she had a feeling that any time spent alone with him would see her decision made quickly.

It was the speed that scared her. It made her feel like she was in a car with no brakes, careening down a mountain. No control, no way to stop. If she was going to be with him she needed control.

Her moment of tranquility was interrupted by the sound of the French doors opening behind her.

"Did you have dinner?" Blaise asked, his footsteps heavy on the stone terrace.

"Yes. I got something from the restaurant in the hotel lobby." Another avoidance tactic she'd used, to great effect.

"Did you enjoy it?"

She looked at him and immediately regretted the action. Her heart slammed into her breast, thundering rapidly, as though it were trying to escape. She couldn't look away, though, because then he would know.

"Of course I enjoyed it. Everyone here does a fabulous job."

"I am glad to hear it."

She found her eyes riveted to his throat, to the up and down motion of his Adam's apple. Even there, he was so different than she was. Fuzzy images drifted through her mind, silken sheets, dark and pale limbs entwined, her lips on that strong throat.

She shook her head, tried to shake off the drugging arousal that was creeping in on her.

She felt like running. To him. Away from him. She

felt like jumping out of her skin, as though her body couldn't contain everything that was swirling around inside of her.

This was what she'd been running from. From what Blaise made her feel.

She was still running. Even after she'd decided not to let fear control her. And now she really *did* want to jump out of her skin. To be someone else. Someone else here with this man who made her feel all of this amazing, burning passion.

But she couldn't. She turned away from Blaise, looked back out at the water, her heart hammering, but for a different reason now.

She couldn't be someone else, and in all probability, her scars looked now as they would look in forty years. They were healed, as much as they would ever be. She'd never accepted that, and she hadn't realized it until now.

Relationships, sex, all of that had seemed like something that would happen later. But she was twenty-five, and it hadn't happened. Because in her mind she had always imagined herself being with a man and looking beautiful, perfect, and while logically she'd always known that would never be, a part of herself had been clinging to the insane hope.

But she wanted Blaise. And he might reject her. So might any man, a man she might not want half as much.

It was now, or not at all. She had to take the step, to claim her life. The fire had taken so much from her. And she was seeing now that she had given it even more than it had taken; she had fed the flames with her fear for the past eleven years, aided by her mother's thoughtless words, by her classmates tormenting her, and she wouldn't do it anymore.

She turned to Blaise again, and she was certain he would be able to see the pulse fluttering at the base of her neck.

She took a step to him, and another, then put her palms flat against his chest. She stood like that, frozen, feeling his heart pound beneath her hands, letting his warmth spread through her.

She slid one hand up, curved it around his neck. He lowered his head slightly and she tilted hers up, capturing his lips. Her heart rate quickened, her breasts felt heavy, her body empty, in need of him. Of Blaise.

She knew what she wanted. The only thing stopping her was fear. Fear couldn't have this. It would take this from her.

Blaise wrapped his arms around her, pulled her in tight, kissing her urgently, hungrily. She wanted to cry. To be wanted, to be held so tightly, as though he were afraid of losing her, it was like balm, healing unseen wounds inside her.

She could feel his desire for her, hard and heavy against her belly. She moved against him, desperately seeking some kind of satisfaction. He lowered one of his hands, cupping her bottom, kneading her flesh. She wiggled against him with more intent, his touch making every part of her burn with need.

"Inside," she said, her voice reflecting her desperation. And she didn't care.

He moved his hand down her thigh, stopping when his hand moved from the bottom of her dress to bare skin, then he pushed the fabric upward. He kissed her temple, her cheek, nipped her earlobe. "I can work with what we have out here."

Out here, in the open. She would feel too exposed. And she didn't possess the knowledge or experience to engage in any sort of serious sexual acrobatics. She didn't really want him to know that.

"Inside," she repeated, lending her voice a commanding note.

She felt his lips curve against her neck. "Whatever you desire."

CHAPTER NINE

BLAISE closed the bedroom door behind them. There was no need—there was no one else in the house, but the action made her feel so much more secure. She wondered if he'd known it would.

"I often wondered if your lips tasted like bubblegum," he said, crossing the room and coming to stand in front of her. He curved his hand around her neck, stroking the back of it with his thumb.

"And?" she asked, breathless.

"They don't," he said, leaning in, kissing her lightly. "They are much richer, more decadent. I cannot place the flavor. It is uniquely you."

"If you had walked into my boutique with some lines like that I might not have been so hostile."

"It is not a line," he said. "It is true."

Her heart tightened and she tried hard to ignore it. This wasn't about her heart. It wasn't about finer emotions. It wasn't for Blaise, and it wouldn't be for her. This was risk enough without introducing anything like that.

"I want you," she said. Because she couldn't think of anything else to say. Her desire for him was pouring through her, it was in her blood, a part of her now.

He moved against her, the evidence of his arousal

clear. She had never been this intimate with a man, had never experienced what it might be like to have a man desire her as Blaise did now.

She placed her hand on his chest again. His heart was raging faster now, stronger. For her. She let her hand drift down, and she could feel the muscle beneath his button-up shirt, could feel the hard-cut definition. She sucked in a sharp breath as her fingers drifted below the waistband of his pants, the tips lightly brushing the solid length of his erection.

He sucked in a breath, his eyes intense on hers. She touched him again, more firmly this time, with more intent, cupping him, testing him.

It wouldn't be so easy to pretend to be experienced. She'd thought she could do it, after all, given her age the likelihood of there being any real physical evidence of her virginity was low. But her basic knowledge of male anatomy hadn't prepared her for Blaise.

You want him. Take him.

She squeezed him lightly, then more firmly and she watched his expression change to one of pure pleasure, a harsh groan escaping his lips.

She abandoned him then, letting her hands drift back up to his shirt collar as she slid one button through its hole at a time, slowly baring his chest to her, his torso. She pushed the shirt off his shoulders and let it fall to the floor.

He was the epitome of male physical perfection. Rich brown skin, well-defined muscles with just enough dark hair sprinkled over them to remind her that he was a man.

Tight, defined ab muscles contracted as he drew in a breath and she could only watch the slight movement of his powerful body with awe. She had known he would be perfect. But she hadn't quite understood how intimidating being faced with the perfection would be.

Never before had she been so conscious of just how lopsided this trade was. He was giving himself, his body, his experience. She was giving him her body, her imperfect, untried body and her knowledge of sexual tips and tricks that were limited to what she'd read in women's magazines.

It was too far to turn back, but a part of her wanted to. Wanted to wrap herself up in her fear and run.

"Can we turn the light off?" she asked.

He pulled her to him, and she pressed her hands against his chest, loving the feel of his bare skin beneath her palms. He kissed her slowly, thoroughly.

"I want to see you," he said softly.

They were the most terrifying words she'd ever heard in her life.

"I don't…you don't."

"Ella," he said, brushing her hair from her face. "I do. But if it makes you more comfortable, I can turn off the lights."

"It's just. I'm sorry, you don't know how bad the rest of the…the rest of my body looks."

"Have your other lovers had problems with your scars?" he asked, anger lacing his voice.

It was the question she had feared. The one she didn't want to answer, because it would expose her, would let him know that the Ella she showed the world was a lie.

It was the question she had to answer now, honestly.

"I haven't had other lovers."

Blaise released his hold on her, his heart pounding hard, from arousal, from shock. "Not possible," he said.

"Very possible," she said, her voice tight.

She had no reason to lie. And yet, it was nearly impossible for him to believe. But he did. He had to. The look on her face, defiance mixed with shame, told him she spoke the truth.

He felt as though he'd been punched in the stomach. This moment was not meant for him; he knew that, emphatically and without doubt. This moment was for a man who could promise Ella love. A commitment. Something other than a few nights of careless pleasure.

He had made up his mind to resist her, to take control of the near mind-numbing desire she aroused in him. And yet, he had not done that. Now she was telling him she was a virgin. Of all his many sins, taking a woman's virginity was not on the list.

He should keep it so. Keep that one blot off his record.

He was acutely aware of the imbalance between them. She was an innocent, of all things, and he...he had been with more women than he could readily tally up. He had followed his own flesh selfishly, had used love as an excuse to take his brother's future wife into his bed.

But this was more than virginity. She hadn't been with a man for a reason, and she had now decided that reason was no longer important. This wasn't a no-strings sexual encounter; it never could have been with Ella. But this...this made it more.

And he had nothing to offer her. Not love. Not commitment. Nothing. He had no right to touch her, no right to seek his own pleasure in her, to feed his own desires with her innocence.

He should go. He should walk away now. Confess his mistake and leave Ella untainted by his hands.

Yet he could not turn away from her. From those wide blue eyes, filled with need, and confusion and fear.

He lifted his hand, and cupped her cheek, the tremble in his fingers likely visible to her. She affected him so strongly, her beauty, her vulnerability. The simple sweetness in her smile, the occasional sharpness of her tongue.

He lowered his hand. It felt hard to do. Heavy.

He tightened his hands into fists. Made the decision to go.

"Blaise." She touched him lightly, her hand on his chest, fingertips exploring him, grazing his nipples. "Please."

"Ella…"

She bit her lip, pink and swollen from the kisses they'd shared, her eyes glittering. Her walls were down, her defenses destroyed. He would be a bastard to take her now. A bastard to leave.

His spot in Hell was already secure, this would only stoke the fire. And he welcomed the burn. He was too far gone now. Too far gone in every way. There was no redeeming him, and there was no stopping the flame of need that had ignited inside him.

He pulled her back to him, kissed her, sliding his hands over her cloth-covered curves. She sighed, let her head fall back. He kissed her, kissed the scar that ran from her shoulder, up her neck and disappeared into her hairline.

She looked at him, eyes wide.

"*Belle*," he said, English deserting him completely for a moment.

"The lights," she whispered, "please."

It took him a moment to translate the meaning of her words, for understanding to penetrate his desire-fogged brain. He pressed a kiss to her forehead before releasing her and walking over to flick the lights off.

Ella let out a breath she hadn't realized she was holding. This would make it easier. He would still feel the damage, but it wouldn't require her to reveal everything to him all at once. Confessing that she was a virgin had been enough. More intimate in some ways than what they were about to do.

She'd thought, for one, gut-wrenching moment that he would leave her when she told him she hadn't been with anyone else. But he hadn't.

When Blaise came back to her, he hesitated before putting his arms around her again and a stab of horror lanced her in the chest. "Don't do this because you feel sorry for me," she said.

He took her chin between his thumb and forefinger. The moon, filtering pale light through the open window, gave her hints of his serious expression. "I am doing this because I want you. So much that my entire body aches with it."

"Mine, too," she whispered.

He placed his mouth next to her ear, whispered every illicit thing he wanted to do with her, while his hands roamed over her body, cupped her breasts, teased her nipples into tight points.

"Blaise." She shuddered, gripping his shoulders as her arousal increased, her body aching with a hollow pain, the need to have him inside of her.

"I'm here," he said, moving his hands to the zipper at the back of her dress.

She closed her eyes as he slid the zipper down. Cool air skimmed over her body as her dress fell to the floor, pooling at her feet. She was still wearing her high heels, and nothing but a small bra and panty set.

She could only see the outline of his body in the dim light, and she imagined that was all he could see of her. She still felt almost overwhelmed, her senses swamped with arousal, need, shame.

She heard the metal sound of his belt buckle being undone, saw him push his pants down his legs and add them to the growing pile of clothes on the floor.

"Stand in front of the window," he said, his voice rough.

The window faced the lake, and she knew no one would see her. She crossed the room and went to stand in front of the glass.

"Beautiful," he whispered. "Take your bra off for me, *cherie.*"

Her fingers trembled as she reached around and unclasped the flimsy article of clothing, freeing her breasts. She gasped as the air hit her sensitized nipples, as she became aware of the full weight of her breasts, longing for Blaise's touch, for his lips, his hands.

"You have such a perfect figure," he said.

She knew the moon was making her silhouette more prominent, outlining her body in a glowing, silver halo, revealing her shape while still concealing her scars. She turned to the side, to give him a different view. He sucked in a sharp breath, loud in the silence of the dim room, and a rush of power and desire assaulted her.

"Come here," he said, another command.

In this situation, she found she enjoyed his commands.

He put his arms around her, drew her to him, and she wanted to simply enjoy the feeling of her bare breasts against his chest, his crisp chest hair teasing her nipples.

Instead she went still when he placed his hands on her back. She closed her eyes as he slid his palms over the worst of her scars. The left side bore the worst of the damage, all of the nerves destroyed. She couldn't feel the fine points of his touch, the texture of his skin, the heat from his palm, she could sense only firm pressure, the weight of his touch, but nothing more.

She waited for him to pull away, to move his hands at least. He had to feel the scars, had to be aware of the dips and craters in her flesh.

He didn't stop touching her, didn't pull his hands away. He went on caressing her, kissing her again, his hot shaft pressed against her belly. When he did move his hands it was so he could shape the outline of her curves, grip her hips and slide her panties down her legs.

She stepped out of them, kicking them to the side.

He put his hands on her hips, got down on his knees. Ella put one hand on his shoulder, one on his head, running her hand lightly over his short hair.

Rough, masculine fingers skimmed her ankle as he worked the tiny buckles on her high-heeled shoes. His thumb massaged her instep as he removed the first shoe, and a shiver moved through her body. She'd never thought the act of shoe removal could ever be erotic, but Blaise took it there. By the time her second shoe had been dispatched, she was shaking, quivering beneath his touch.

He caressed the back of her knees with his hands, leaned in and kissed her there and she was shocked when a lightning bolt of need crashed through her. He worked his way upward, kissing a trail up to her inner thigh. Hot lips pressed against the tender skin and she let her head fall back on a sigh.

When he moved his lips to a more intimate place, licking, kissing, sucking, she moved both hands to his shoulders, clinging to him so that she didn't fall over.

Her thighs started shaking, waves of pleasure washing over her. Just before she could reach the peak he pulled back, pulled away and stood. Desire gnawed at her, unfulfilled, unsatisfied.

He led her to the bed and she went gladly. He opened the nightstand drawer and pulled out a condom packet, placing it on the pillow beside her head. He moved his hand between her legs, stroking her, drawing wetness up and slicking his thumb over her clitoris.

She moaned, her muscles tightening, contracting. He continued to stroke her as he penetrated her with one finger, testing her. He added a second, stretching her slightly, making sure she was ready.

Everything in her was strung tight, she could hardly breathe, her body poised on the brink of cracking beneath the building pleasure. Her orgasm crashed over her suddenly, like a wave, swallowing her whole and carrying her, weightless and breathless to the shore.

He kissed her, reaching for the condom packet, opened it quickly and rolled it on deftly. "Ready?" He asked.

She nodded. She was ready. She was replete, and yet she still wanted more. Still wanted him. Inside her.

He entered her slowly, allowing her body time to stretch to accommodate him. It didn't hurt, she simply felt full. Deliciously so.

She gripped his shoulders again, let her head fall back. He kissed her, deeply, passionately as he began to move inside her.

She was surprised by how quickly the pleasure started to build in her again, how fast he was able to bring her to the edge again, panting, clawing at his back. His movements became uncontrolled, as hers did, as she rocked against him, seeking her own pleasure as she gave all that she knew how to give to him.

"Blaise," she said hoarsely when her second climax hit, deeper this time, the pleasure starting at her center and radiating out.

He thrust into her one last time, freezing above her as he found his own release, his shaft pulsing within her as he gave himself up to it, overtaken as she had been. She held him to her, her hands splayed across his sweat-slicked back, his heart pounding heavily against her chest. She didn't want to move, didn't want to face the reality of what had happened between them.

She just wanted to revel in the moment. Revel in being connected to someone. Connected to Blaise.

He withdrew after a moment, rolling over and climbing out of bed. She stayed as she was, unable to move. He walked into the bathroom and returned a few moments later, climbing back in beside her.

Relief swept over her. He would stay with her.

Tonight, he was hers.

And she wasn't afraid.

Blaise could only stare at Ella's back as the morning light filtered in through the window, casting a harsh ray of sun over the affected skin. She was still asleep, her back to him, the sheet she was covered in riding low on her hips, exposing her entire upper body and the rounded curves of her butt. And the scars. His first instinct was to touch, but he held back. Not for fear of hurting her, just out of respect.

He had touched them last night, had felt the uneven skin beneath his fingertips. He had imagined, fantasized, about running hands over her smooth skin. There was so much of her skin that wasn't smooth.

Uneven coloring, pockets and craters covered the landscape of her back. It spoke of trauma, it spoke of pain. Pain so deep, so real, it made his chest ache.

But even with the stark difference between Ella and every other woman he'd been with, she had lived up to every expectation. Sex with Ella had been pleasure beyond anything he'd ever known. She had stripped him of his control, of his ability to think straight.

He had lost control, for the second time in his life. He didn't like the man it made him then, he liked the man he was now even less. To take Ella's virginity when he had nothing for her. It was more than that. It was the fact that her facade was a lie. The fact that she truly didn't wear her scars like trophies, as he had once thought she did.

What she showed the world was a shield. To keep people from looking too closely.

She hid the worst of them. The worst of her pain. And when she had revealed the fact that she'd never been with a man last night, she had revealed that her scars went well beneath the surface of her skin.

And he did not possess the power to heal them. All he had ever done for those in his life was cause pain. He had caused his mother pain by reminding her of his father, had caused his brother pain by taking the woman he loved for his own. He had even caused Marie pain in the end.

It would only continue with Ella. Like an infection, he spread the worst of himself to each person who touched his life. He had hurt his father by going with his mother, had hurt his mother in a way, by enabling her to come back to Malawi, where she had died because of their inability to get to a proper medical facility. And his brother...he had destroyed Luc.

It was why he had stopped trying. Why he had cut off his emotions, embraced his ability to be ruthless and single-minded in his pursuits, mixing it with control to keep himself distant from anyone who cared about him.

Not last night, though. There had been no control then. There wasn't any more control now. He had stopped noticing guilt a long time ago. It was a constant companion and he had grown immune to the gnawing sensation of it.

But this morning, he felt it, so strong it was as if physical weight had been placed on his chest.

Still he didn't move.

He reached out and ran his fingertips over her skin, memorizing the way it felt beneath his hands. The pain and suffering the marks represented were beyond what he could understand in a physical sense.

They were beyond what anyone should be expected to endure. Least of all a woman like Ella.

"Blaise?" She sat up suddenly, her back still to him, her head bent low as she tried to gather up the sheet around her shoulders.

"No, don't." He sat up, reached around her, captured her hands in his, lowering them slowly, and with them, the sheet.

If fell around her waist, and she sat there, her spine held rigid, her muscles trembling beneath his touch. He flattened his palms against her back, slid them down, back up again.

"They don't hurt, do they?"

She shook her head. "No." Her voice sounded strangled.

"Was anyone else injured in the fire?"

"No." Just no. Nothing else. But that single word held a wealth of pain.

"How bad was it?"

"I was in the hospital for a few months. The same walls. Horrible food. And the pain. And then there were the skin grafts. So many surgeries. Recovery from burns is worse than getting the burns in the first place. At least, it was for me."

Her head was still bent down, her shoulders bunched tight. He put his hands on her shoulders, slid them down her arms, repeating the motion until he felt her relax beneath his hands.

"I have extensive nerve damage," she said, her voice soft. "I don't have feeling on the left side of my back. The scar on my neck…it's the same. I have no feeling there."

He bent his head, his forehead resting against her back, between her shoulder blades. Pain lancing his chest.

"Then I will have to kiss you twice as much on the right side, to make up for it," he said.

Ella's heart felt like it would pound out of her chest, tears stinging her eyes as she bit her lip in hopes of keeping them from falling.

Last night with Blaise had gone so far beyond anything she'd ever imagined possible for her. And he was still here. In the full light of day he was still in bed with her, touching her. Saying the most romantic things she'd ever heard in her life.

"I would be a fool to turn down that offer," she said, her voice trembling.

"I would be, too." He paused for a moment, pressing a kiss to her shoulder. "I don't want to hurt you, Ella."

The admission seemed torn from him, as though it pained him to admit something good and decent about himself.

"You didn't hurt me. You won't. You…I never imagined any man would want me." It hurt to admit that. To admit that she'd allowed her tormentors at school, her mother's comments spawned from her own guilt, to poison her so much.

"I…this boy in school asked me on a date. I was eighteen. He took me parking, you know? And he put his hand under my shirt. And he felt my back. That was the end of the parking and he told…he told everyone that I was disfigured. Hideous."

Blaise bit out a foul curse in his native language. "If I ever met the man, I would not be held responsible for what I did to him."

There was more. But she couldn't admit that. Couldn't possibly let him know the extent of it. It was too humiliating. Being made to feel second-rate by classmates was one thing. It happened to so many people. But experiencing it at the hands of her own mother…that was what she carried closest to her heart.

"It doesn't matter now." She took a breath. "I didn't want to be afraid anymore." She turned to face him, not bothering to cover her breasts with the sheet. It had been much more intimate, much more difficult to show him her back. "And I'm not. I feel like I just won something, in fact."

Blaise looked at Ella's radiant smile, at her pink tinged cheeks. Such an odd choice of words she'd used. Like she'd won something. Because he felt like he was losing something. Something he was desperate to hold on to.

CHAPTER TEN

ELLA wasn't happy about having to get out of bed. She wanted to stay there, wrapped in the sheets, tangled in Blaise.

But it was day two of the photo shoot and duty called.

She thought of Blaise, though, while she watched Carolina posing beneath the waterfall in full formalwear. When she was with Blaise, she felt real confidence. Real happiness. He made her feel beautiful.

A laugh bubbled up in her throat and the photo shoot director turned to give her a hard look. As though he thought she was laughing at him. The man was an *artiste*. He possessed no sense of humor and more than his fair share of narcissism. But the laughter had nothing to do with him.

Beautiful. She hadn't felt beautiful in eleven years. There had been a time when she'd been a part of the in crowd, the golden girl from a golden family. Until the fire had burned it all away. No one had known what to do with the lasting effects of the blaze. No one had known how to react to her.

So they had made her an object of ridicule.

But today, she felt some of that melt away.

The warm breeze kissed her face, and she smiled. She

was finally taking control. No, she hadn't asked for the scars, and if she had the choice, she wouldn't pick them, but she'd spent so many years being angry because of the fire. Shaking her fist at the sky because it wasn't fair.

It still wasn't. But it was the way things were. It was her life.

And last night she had taken the first step to making herself a life that had some balance, that wasn't so controlled by an event that had happened so long ago. A step to finding freedom.

Control had been the name of the game for so long. But it was a tightly controlled prison. It didn't allow anyone in, and it only allowed pieces of her out. Only allowed her to feel and experience certain things.

Since meeting Blaise her focus had started to expand, and after last night…it was as though a veil had been ripped from her eyes. It made her face, really face, how much she had held herself back.

It was more than that, though. Being with Blaise had changed something, something inside of her. She felt alive, excited about life. About more than just work. It was like waking up.

As long as it didn't grow into more. It wouldn't. Blaise had been…good to her. But he was a practiced seducer, and that's what he was doing with her: seducing her. She didn't mind it, because that was what she wanted.

But she would have to be an idiot to fall in love with a man who was such a bad bet. And while she'd been called a whole host of very insulting things, that wasn't one of them.

"I'm back," Ella called when she walked into the villa. It was late, the sun was sinking into the lake and she was starving.

Blaise didn't answer.

She wandered around the sitting room, and then sat on the plush velvet couch. There was a folded piece of paper on the side table and she picked it up. It was a note, from Blaise, and written in surprisingly elegant handwriting.

Dinner. On the lake.

Elegant handwriting, but a very masculine missive. No hearts or frills for Blaise Chevalier. She smiled.

She had gotten hot and sweaty during the photo shoot, but she was too hungry to change before eating. It was a desperate matter, in her mind. Some women might be able to skip a meal now and then, but she wasn't one of them.

She had on a nice sundress anyway, the kind that showed her legs. Blaise seemed to like them. She smiled as she headed out the back door of the villa.

Blaise was there, his white shirt untucked and open at the collar, a single rose in his hand. It was a small thing, the rose, but it made her stomach tighten. The last time she'd gotten flowers she'd been in a hospital bed.

There was a large white boat moored on the dock. The place where their dinner awaited. A yacht and a rose.

"I wish I would have dressed up."

"You always look beautiful," he said, walking toward her, his hand outstretched.

She took the rose from him and lifted it to her face, brushing the velvet petals over her cheek lightly as she inhaled the delicate scent. "Thank you," she said.

"Hold on to it, I have plans for that rose later."

"That sounds…like it has the possibility of being a little bit naughty."

A wicked grin parted his lips. "I never claimed to be nice."

No, he hadn't. But he certainly did a good impression of a nice man on occasion. And that was what confused her.

Because she was well acquainted with Blaise the corporate raider, and the media version of Blaise: the rabid womanizer and ruthless thief of his brother's fiancée. And she had just met the man who had deep roots in his mother's homeland, who did so much to make it a better place. Even more recently she'd met Blaise, the lover. The man who touched her scars without flinching, who invited her to dinner on a yacht.

And she had the terrible feeling that it was Blaise, her lover, who was in danger of evaporating one day.

But until then, she would make the most of every possible minute with him.

"How was the shoot?" he asked, his hand on the small of her back, guiding her to the dock.

"Great. Better today. It's…it's funny. I was so concerned about maintaining my control, and I'm now facing the reality that there are so many people involved in the making of a career. Models, directors, stylists, and I'm only a piece. I create the clothes, but it's not all up to me."

"You imagined it would be?"

"Yes, I think I did. I mean, I knew that all of those people would have roles, but I hadn't considered how every person who touches the gown makes it slightly different than it was when I created it, either through the pose they choose or the way they style it."

"And are you okay with that?"

"Yesterday, I didn't think I would be. But today I saw why a collaboration works, and I was happy. I let go, and that's not something I like to do, but it was rewarding."

She took a deep breath of the heavy, fragrant air. "That's one reason I was so put off by you."

"But only one reason," he said, lacing his fingers with hers as he led her up the gangplank and onto the yacht.

"Well, there were several reasons," she said absently, her heart expanding as she looked at the surroundings.

There were candles placed near a plush, velvet blanket that was spread out on the deck, surrounded by large, jewel tone throw pillows. There was a classic, woven picnic basket set off to the side, and two wineglasses near an opened bottle of white.

"There were…there were reasons," she said, smiling slightly.

"And what were they?"

"They've slipped my mind," she said. "Because if you had brought this out the first night we met, I think I would have warmed to you more quickly."

"Ah, so you can be bought."

"With a picnic on a private yacht? Yeah." She turned and smiled at him and her heart tightened when she saw him smiling back. A real smile. It was such a rare thing to see on his handsome face. Sometimes it seemed his face was chiseled into that set, impassive expression.

Not right now. Not with her.

"Shameless," he said, drawing her to him, his fingers tangling in her hair.

"Maybe." She felt breathless now, with him so close. She wanted him to kiss her, wanted to lose herself in the sensual mastery of his touch. It had been too long. Way too long.

"I think you need food more than you need a kiss."

Did she? She'd thought so a few minutes earlier, but

now, now that she was with him, she was changing her mind. "I don't know about that."

"I do. You were out in the heat all day, and you probably didn't take an adequate lunch break."

"I got too involved to stop and eat."

"I'm not surprised."

"Don't even accuse me of being a workaholic, Blaise Chevalier, because I would just turn that one right around back to you."

"I wasn't going to deny being a workaholic. Tonight, though, I think I will leave work where it belongs, *oui?*"

"I will, too."

Blaise sat on the blanket and she joined him. It was getting dark now, the streaks of orange from the setting sun fading into a dusky gold, the air turning purple around them. There were no streetlights, nothing to interfere with the emerging moon and stars.

Blaise poured them each a half glass of wine and Ella opened the basket and pulled out a platter of meat, cheese and fruit.

"Lovely," she said, picking up a piece of salami and taking a bite. She noticed Blaise looking at her and she narrowed her eyes. "What? I'm hungry, remember?"

"I'm glad. Eat."

"Don't stare then!" she said, laughing, unable to stop the bubble of joy from escaping her lips. She felt happy. She noticed because it wasn't very often she felt completely content right where she was. She always looked to the future, to goals she had yet to achieve. Not now. Now she was just living in the moment.

He smiled, at her, making her feel like she was the only woman on the planet. "I am only staring because you're so beautiful."

She bit her lip, her stomach tightening a touch, dimming the joy she'd felt a moment earlier. "I don't know how you can say that."

His dark brows locked together. "You don't know how I can think you're beautiful?"

She shook her head, setting the meat down on the plate. "No. I don't."

"Then I will tell you," he said, eyes intent on hers. "You have such beautiful eyes, expressive, deep. And your lips…a man could weave fantasies about your lips. I know I have." He reached his hand out and stroked his thumb over her lower lip, slowly, gently. "What they would feel like against my skin, how they would taste, and I am not disappointed."

He slid his hand down, fingers skimming her collarbone and down further, teasing her tightening nipples. "Your breasts fit in my hands so perfectly, your whole body is shaped just as a woman's body should be. As though you were molded in my dreams."

She could feel her face burning, her heart racing. The words, such perfect, sincere words, spoken in that deep, seductive voice, resonated through her. It was difficult to believe. Impossible in some ways. And yet, his eyes were on fire with the truth of it.

She blinked, tears assaulting her again. That seemed to happen with Blaise. She'd spent the past eleven years cultivating her defenses, ensuring no one ever knew they affected her, making absolutely certain that no one ever saw the weakness in her.

But Blaise had demolished her defenses, left her open and vulnerable. And for some reason, she didn't feel weaker for it. In some ways she felt stronger.

He took his hand away, picked up his wine and turned

his attention to dinner. The silence between them wasn't awkward, it was companionable. Comfortable.

"Thank you," she said softly, satisfied by the food, happy to be with him. His words echoed in her, reverberating through her.

She cleared her throat, still fighting not to cry. "This is so nice."

"You need to relax more, Ella. Come here." He patted the blanket in front of him and she moved so that she was sitting with her back to him, his powerful thighs bracketing her.

He moved his hands to her shoulders, kneaded away some of the tension. She couldn't remember the last time someone had done that for her. She'd never paid anyone to give her a massage because that would require her showing the parts of herself she hadn't come to terms with.

But Blaise had seen the worst now. He knew what was beneath her fashionable dresses and cool demeanor. And he was still here. He could still touch her.

She felt his hand on the zipper of her dress, felt it sliding down, exposing her skin to the warm evening air. Blaise kissed her neck, first her scar, then the other side, twice. "No one can see us here," he whispered.

He pushed the thin straps of her dress down, baring her breasts, her back, entirely. "How much sensation have you lost?" he asked.

"Close to half of my back has nerve damage," she said. "My arms aren't as bad—they have feeling at least, even the left one."

"I see." He leaned sideways, picking up the rose from where she'd set in on the blanket. "Do you feel this?"

The sensation of soft, velvet petals skimmed over her neck, the top of her shoulder.

"Yes," she said, "Blaise, what…"

"I want to know where you can feel my touch. How I can best pleasure you. I want to know your body." She felt the rose, guided by Blaise's hand, gliding softly over her skin. "Can you feel this?"

"Yes," she whispered.

A breeze blew in off the surface of the water, the sharp cold and her near unbearable arousal tightening her nipples to painful peaks.

He moved the rose lower and her sense of it evaporated. "And here, Ella?"

"No," she said, her throat tight. She wished she could feel him. All of him. Everywhere. The fact that her body denied that filled her with frustration.

Then his touch was there again, cool and featherlight at the base of her spine. "There. I can feel you there," she whispered.

"Here?" She felt the petals skim across her lower back.

"Yes, *oh, yes,*" she sighed, her body aching for more of his touch, for a firmer touch. And yet, she was enjoying the tease, the sensual torture. There was no more frustration, only need. Only the desire to be with Blaise again. To be joined to him.

"And this?" he asked. She felt his lips, hot and firm against her shoulder blade. She felt the sensation down to her core, internal muscles clenching tight as her heart rate increased.

She could only nod, biting her lip to keep a moan of pleasure from escaping. Her entire body shuddered and she didn't even try to hold back her sounds of approval when she felt the tip of his tongue trace the line of her spine.

"I felt all of that," she said, her throat so constricted it was hard to force the words out.

"Here," he said, his fingers drifting to a place she could no longer feel. "This is where the worst of the damage is." He leaned in again and even though she couldn't see, she knew he'd kissed her there.

A tear spilled down her cheek and she didn't bother to brush it away.

"But here." He kissed her on her shoulder. "Here you feel me?"

"Yes," she whispered, closing her eyes.

"I have a map of you now," he said, his fingers drifting over her.

She wanted to tell him that he now knew her body better than she did, but she couldn't speak for fear she'd dissolve completely into tears.

So she turned and kissed him instead, pouring every ounce of her emotion into it. He kissed her back, his hands moving now to cup her breasts, tease her nipples.

"Oh, I was waiting for that," she sighed and let her head fall back.

"So was I," he said, nipping her lip lightly and soothing the sting away with his tongue.

"You're overdressed," she said, touching his chest.

"I can remedy that."

He made quick work of his clothes, discarding them onto the deck. She ran her hands over his chest, over his perfect, unblemished skin, his tight, muscular form. "You're so perfect," she murmured.

He caught her hand, kissed the tender underside of her wrist. "No more than you."

Tears assaulted her again and she blinked them back, determined not to cry now, not when she craved release so very much. And crying would certainly destroy the mood of sensual intimacy that surrounded them.

She only wished she could give to him, as he had to her. What he had done was more than a sexy exercise, more than simple foreplay. He had touched her, looked at her, brought the part of herself she was most ashamed of into the affair, rather than ignoring it, or tolerating it.

He had taken the time to learn her body. All of it.

She stood for a moment, shimmying out of her dress and underwear, kicking her shoes off and idly hoping she was able to find them in the dim evening light.

She dropped to her knees, kissing his chest, running her tongue over his perfectly sculpted pecs. She craved him, more than food or drink, was suddenly driven by the need to taste him. She traced a line down the center of his torso and she felt his muscles contract sharply beneath her touch.

She gripped the thick, hard length of him in her hand, then dipped her head lower still, hoping she could give him half the pleasure tonight as he'd given her the night before. It was her turn to explore. Her turn to learn.

One of his hands gripped her shoulder, the other, forked through her hair, his masculine groans of pleasure fueling her own desire. That she could make his muscles tremble, bring him to the brink of sexual ecstasy, was a heady rush she'd never anticipated.

"Ella," he rasped, his voice strained. "Enough, *ma belle*. I need all of you now."

She lifted her head, could see his eyes, glittering with desire, the stars reflected in them. "I need all of you," she said, pushing lightly on his chest. He leaned back against the pillows, giving to her slight physical command. "Condom?"

He grinned wickedly, white teeth shining in the moonlight as he reached beneath one of the pillows and produced a packet. She took it from his hand, tearing it open.

"So sure of yourself?" she asked.

"I did provide you with dinner on a yacht," he said, still smiling.

And so much more. "Yes, you did."

She fumbled with the condom for a moment, allowing him to place his hand over hers to help her roll it onto his length.

"I'll figure it out next time," she said.

"I'm not complaining at all." He placed his hand on her cheek, kissed her lightly on the lips as his other hand cupped her buttocks, urged her to come nearer to him, to straddle his body as the kiss intensified.

She positioned herself above him, moving until she could feel the blunt head of his erection pressing against the entrance to her body. She lowered herself onto him slowly, her breath hissing through her teeth as he filled her.

"Good?" she asked.

He tightened his hold on her rear. "Yes."

She started to move over him, finding her rhythm, the one that made her body pulse and made Blaise's eyes close in ecstasy. His hands roamed over her back, traced the path where she was able to feel him expertly.

"Beautiful," he grated. "So beautiful."

His words, the movement of his hands, of his body, pushed her over the edge, her orgasm overtaking her, radiating through her body with all the force of a tremor. Shaking her, rocking her to her core.

He tightened his hold on her, gripped her tightly around the waist and reversed their positions, keeping himself buried deep inside her. He set the pace now, seeking his own release, still adding to her pleasure.

And when he found his release, she was hit with an aftershock, more mild than the first, a slower roll of pleasure that seemed to grow as it fed off his. She looked up at the stars, watched as they seemed to rain down over her.

She gripped his shoulders tight, kissed his collarbone.

He rolled to the side, his arms encircling her. She rested her hand on his chest, sheltered her face in the curve of his neck.

"I didn't need the yacht or the picnic," she whispered. "This was enough."

Blaise's body still ached for Ella, even after the most explosive sex of his life. He wanted more. And even when he'd had it, he was certain his satisfaction would last for only a moment before the need to have her grew to near unbearable levels again.

He stroked his hand over her side, skimming the indent of her waist, the curve of her hip. She was unique, in so many ways. He could never mistake her for another woman. An innocent siren, perfect and yet damaged. She was a study in contradiction, and she fascinated him endlessly.

It was a new feeling. Women were indistinct in his mind, his past sexual encounters blurring together. Especially the ones that had happened just after Marie left him.

Marie was distinct still. But with her it had been a need to possess, to claim her for himself. He'd long since realized that what he'd felt for her hadn't been love. He'd stopped believing in the emotion, or at least in his ability to truly experience it.

What he had with Ella felt different. It wasn't about mere possession. He wanted to give to her. To know her body as intimately as possible so he could give her the pleasure she deserved to get from her lover.

Of course, any gift from him was something of a poison chalice.

And even with that realization, he didn't release her. He continued to hold her, continued to stroke the contours of her body.

"No one except for doctors and nurses have ever touched my scars like that," she said, her voice muted. "After the fire…my mother couldn't even touch me anymore."

He clenched his jaw tight. His own mother had struggled with the same issue, and then his father later. He had been caught in the middle of a bitter divorce, and as good to him as his mother had been, as passionate as she had been about taking him to Malawi with her, there were moments when he reminded her too much of his father. And when he'd returned to France at the age of sixteen, after his mother's death, his father had seen too much of his mother in him, and had seen the son who'd left him.

"A reflection of her own issues," he said tightly, "not yours."

"I understand that. Now. I'm starting to anyway."

"What happened, Ella?"

He felt a hot tear roll from her cheek and drop onto his chest. His stomach tightened. He didn't do well with female tears. But Ella didn't sob, didn't give any indication she was crying other than the moisture she left on his skin.

"My family lived in upstate New York in this huge manor home. It was like a maze. Three stories, thousands of square feet and a lot of rooms. We were all asleep. By the time we woke up…it was so hot." Her voice was distant, as though she were relaying secondhand information, not talking about something that had happened to her personally. "The knob on my bedroom door burned my hand." She held out her left hand, traced the nearly invisible crescent of wrinkled skin on that palm. "I was too scared to jump from a third-floor window so I tried to just…walk out."

He tightened his hold on her, a sick feeling hitting him. Seeing Ella's scars, he knew there had been pain, and he was conscious of that fact every time he saw them. But to hear of it, that was something different.

He was helpless to do anything but listen. He hated the feeling. Hated that he had nothing to give her. Mostly he hated that it had happened to her. He had set the fire in his own life, and his consequences were his own. Ella had done nothing to earn such suffering.

"How did you get out?" he asked.

"The second-story window. I tried to get down the stairs to the front but it was…consumed and I was already burned from trying to make it down the hallway… I couldn't breathe anymore."

"Your family?" he asked, his throat tight.

"Was safe. They were on the lawn, all clinging to each other."

"They had gone into my sister's room and gotten her out first and then…they couldn't come back inside for me." Another tear landed on his chest. "And it is terrible of me to wonder why it went that way. To feel angry that they didn't risk their lives for me."

"But you do."

Silence settled between them and he sensed the struggle in her, the war that raged in her body.

"Yes," she whispered. "I have spent my life trying to prove I was worthy of the sacrifice they wouldn't give to me. But it doesn't matter. It doesn't change anything. They can't…they can hardly look at me because they blame themselves, too, and…and they can't handle their guilt."

"And you're not allowed to be angry."

She shook her head.

"I'm sorry, Ella," he said, the words torn from him. "You are worth more than that." It was the absolute truth. She was worth more than a family that couldn't put away their own guilt to help Ella heal. She was worth more than a man who could offer her nothing more than physical pleasure in the bedroom.

Her family was too selfish to see outside of their own pain and into Ella's. And he was too selfish to let her go.

"What about your family?" she asked. "Do you see them now."

"Yes," he said. "Sometimes."

"Your brother?"

His hands tightened slowly into fists. "Yes."

She paused for a moment as if waiting for him to go on. "That's good," she said.

"We're going back to Paris tomorrow."

"I know," she whispered.

"You sound sad."

"I kind of like the yacht." She laughed, the sound shaky still, her voice thick with the remaining tears.

He let his fingers drift from her arm to her collarbone, down to her breasts, tracing lightly around her taut nipple. "I have yachts in France."

CHAPTER ELEVEN

As soon as they were back on French soil, Ella started seeing evidence of the effects of their time in Malawi. Tabloids had photos of them, standing together on the beach at Lake Nyasu for the photo shoot, Blaise's hand resting on her lower back in a casually intimate manner.

And the morning the story had hit the lifestyle pages, her boutique had been slammed with customers, all looking to see if they could find the white shift dress Ella had been wearing on the beach that day. Fortunately it had been stocked and it had translated to sales. It had also meant that owners of other boutiques had been calling, trying to find out if they could get her clothing in their larger stores.

It was the kind of thing that Ella had only ever imagined happening to her before, but it was happening now. The fact that she got to share it with Blaise only made it better.

Blaise. She couldn't think of him without a smile curving her lips. Her lover. The man who held her in his arms at night, the man who looked at her body with desire in his eyes rather than revulsion or detachment.

Ella finished placing and sizing the last photo in her virtual portfolio and readied it to send on to Statham's department store. The massive retail chain had requested a chance to look at her more commercial pieces.

That was the biggest boon of all. And the ad campaign for *Look,* featuring her designs, hadn't even been released yet. She couldn't even imagine what might happen when it was.

Getting her line in such a prominent chain of stores would be the beginning of her being a household name. It would be the beginning of her feeling valid. Of her proving that she was worth it. That it was worth it for her to be alive. To prove that to her mother.

And yet, she found it just didn't matter in that way anymore.

She was proud of the accomplishment, thrilled that it had come from the work she'd done with Blaise. Pleased that something she was passionate about was being received well. But it wasn't about proving her worth anymore.

Because she felt like she was worth something. She had been validated by industry professionals and consumers.

And then there was Blaise.

They'd been back for two days and she hadn't had a chance to see him. She missed him. Missed his touch, his kiss, his possession. She curled her toes in her boots and hit Send on the email, with her portfolio attached, to Statham's.

She leaned back in her office chair, her heart thundering in her chest. She'd been a virgin for twenty-five years and she'd managed to bear it. Now, after two days without Blaise she felt like she might explode with pent-up sexual energy.

But he was busy. She was busy. She'd had a lot to catch up on with the boutique, and the different portfolio and meeting requests. But she was caught up now, until more came in.

She shouldn't call him. Not until he called her. She really shouldn't.

Snatching her mobile phone from the desk, she hit the speed dial for Blaise's number and chewed her bright pink thumbnail, heart thundering in her temples as it rang.

"Ella."

She shivered when he said her name, his voice as affecting, as sinfully delightful now as it had been the first time she'd heard it. No, more now. Because now she'd heard it whispering all the intimate, delicious things he wanted to do to her body. And better still, she had the experience of him being a man of his words.

"Hi. I was just…I know I've been really busy, but I just sent off the last of my unfinished business."

She waited. Waited for him to take the hint and say he wanted to see her. This was almost more terrifying than the first time he'd seen her scarred skin. Because she was showing him more than just her external imperfections. She was giving him a look into her, into her feelings.

Feelings she wasn't certain had a place in her life, or in his.

He didn't say anything, so she pressed on. "I was wondering if you wanted to see me tonight?"

"I'm attending a social gathering tonight," he said, his voice closed off.

"A party."

"A gathering of people."

"Yeah, a party." She gripped her phone tightly, her palm slick with sweat. "You don't want to take me?" It was a stupid question. Stupid to let her insecurity show like that. Stupid to *be* so insecure.

"I didn't think you would be interested. I'm going to talk business."

"And if I had a business social function to attend would you expect to go with me?"

"Yes," he said, without hesitation.

"Can you say 'double standard'?"

"Double standard," he said wryly. "I didn't say I was right, I simply said I would expect to go with you."

"You implied that you were right," she said acidly, "because you always think you're right."

"True."

She blew out a breath. "Okay, I know that what we're doing here isn't a permanent thing. I know that this is physical. But in my mind, it's a relationship. I was a virgin because of the scars, because I was so afraid to be rejected because of them. But I think, even without them, I would have taken a sexual relationship seriously. And that means I sort of expect to be the date to things." Her stomach tightened. "You aren't taking someone else with you, are you?"

"I see no point in playing two women at once. If I want a woman, I take her. If I do not, I break it off with her," he said, his tone hard, more like the Blaise she'd first met than her fantasy lover of the past week.

But she'd insulted him, she realized that. She'd accused him of cheating, basically, and she had no reason to do so. "Sorry. But you have to admit, not telling me about something like this seems a little shady from my perspective."

"It was not my intent to be—" he seemed to be searching for a word "—shady. But I keep my business life and my personal life separate."

"Except when you're managing my business."

"What has happened between us was unavoidable. Normally I would not sleep with a business associate."

"I feel all warm inside now," she said, her voice flat.

"Are you determined to start a fight?"

"No. I'm sorry."

"How do I make you happy now?" he asked, frustration edging his voice.

She laughed. "It's not…I'm not trying to be petulant and get my way. You go to the party by yourself if you want to. I just felt excluded. If I'm a two-night stand then tell me, but I was assuming that we were going to continue on."

"You're not a two-night stand," he said roughly.

Her thoughts wandered back to the night on the yacht, when he'd drifted the rose over her body, his fingers following, as he learned the map of her body, how to touch her. No, it was more than a simple fling, she was sure of that. She just wasn't sure Blaise wanted it to be more.

"And you're not ashamed of me?"

"*Mon dieu!* Ella, no I am not ashamed of you." He sounded genuinely affronted by that.

"Sorry again. My own family was, though. My parents wouldn't allow me to wear a normal swimsuit when we went to the Country Club. I had to wear one that was styled like the Olympic swimmers wear."

Silence hung between them. Again, she'd said too much. She'd told him things she'd never told another soul before. But she longed to get it out now, longed to purge herself of it and be done with it.

"Ella, I don't know what you want from me," he said slowly.

"Honesty," she said, her throat tight. "I'll take honesty."

"And I'll give it to you."

"Thank you."

"I'll talk to you later."

Ella nodded, even though he couldn't see, and pressed the End Call button on her phone.

Blaise swore loudly into the empty silence of his office. It did nothing to make him feel better. Ella made him feel like the inside of his chest was bleeding sometimes. To realize she thought him ashamed of her, to know why she felt that way, because of her family and the clumsy way they had dealt with the aftermath of the fire.

He wasn't the right man to handle her. He had tried to distance himself since their return to Paris, in an effort to cool things between them, in an effort to stop before she got hurt. Before he hurt her.

But then she'd called, her siren's voice luring him to the rocks again.

He'd been so close to asking her to come with him tonight anyway. But he would not be manipulated. Marie had been a master of manipulating him. And he had allowed it.

He would not allow Ella to do the same.

Most of his relationships in the past three years had been brief one- or two-night encounters, and he didn't want that with Ella. He wasn't through with her yet. Just the thought of her had him hard and aching to be in her again. He was dying for the taste, the touch of her, to be sheathed in her tight, wet body while they were both driven to the peak.

But she was working at his control. He recognized that. He couldn't allow it.

No. He held the cards in their relationship. There was no question. And he wanted Ella. Tonight. He wanted her by his side at the party, and he wanted her in his bed later.

And he would have her.

"It was a mistake, to think I would be better off without you for the evening."

Ella blushed beneath Blaise's rather intimate appraisal. Mostly because she still felt ashamed for acting so transparent earlier, and for essentially begging herself a spot as his date for the night.

But when he'd called back less than twenty minutes after their initial conversation she'd been hard-pressed to say no when he'd asked her to go with him. It would just seem way too contrary and ridiculous to refuse after making such a big deal of it. She only wished she hadn't said anything.

It had been honest, though. She wasn't in this relationship lightly. Even if it was only sexual. It had been huge for her to open up to him, to show him her body, to let him touch her, caress her. Revealing her physical self to him had been the beginning of revealing all of herself.

Blaise wore his scars on the inside, and that afforded a kind of protection she didn't have. Blaise knew more about her than anyone else on the planet, and she couldn't help but feel like she had some claim on him because of that.

He didn't share with her. Nothing but his body.

She'd tried to find out about his family when they'd been on the yacht, but she'd only gotten simple, one word answers that had left her with nothing real to go on. It bothered her more than she wanted to admit, because he had gotten hold of her heart.

"Thank you for the almost-compliment," she said, tight lipped as he led her into the ballroom of the luxury hotel.

He was meeting with a potential client, someone he was interested in investing in. Someone who was hesitant to get Blaise involved thanks to his reputation, so he'd told her on the limo ride over.

He gripped her arm and turned her to face him. "It was a compliment. I made a mistake. What more do you want?"

"Nothing," she said. "Except for you to have thought to ask me in the first place." She winced as soon as the words left her mouth.

"I did think of it," he said, his voice low, eyes intent on hers. "But this is a business meeting as far as I'm concerned and I need to concentrate." His gaze flickered over her and she became acutely conscious of just how short and tight her gown was. And she warmed when she saw the heated approval reflected in the golden depths of his eyes. "I do not need to walk around so turned on I can scarcely see straight."

She felt the corners of her lips turn up.

"You enjoy that?" he asked.

"Crude as compliments come, but yes, I enjoyed it a little bit."

Far better to have him not want her here because she was a distraction than to have him not want her here because he was bored with her already.

"Glad to hear it."

"Somehow, I don't think you are."

"Oh, I am." Blaise took her arm and turned her to him, seemingly unfazed by the people that were watching them with rapt interest. "What man doesn't want to hear that he's satisfied his lover?"

"Am I your lover?" she asked.

Blaise dipped his head, his lips skimming her cheek as he leaned in. "Do you not remember?" he whispered.

A sensual shiver crawled over Ella's skin, reached into her and made her entire body tighten at the memory of his touch, his kiss. Of course she remembered. She could do nothing else.

"It's hard to remember since it's been so long," she said, trying to keep her voice steady.

"Has it?"

"I thought you might have lost interest."

His lips flattened, his eyes growing distant. "I don't do the insecure-female thing, Ella."

Anger ignited in her, just as hot as the longing it replaced. "This isn't the 'insecure-female thing.' This is me not being appreciative of the lack of contact. I'm not needy, but I do expect some respect."

"Have I ever given you a reason to believe I disrespect you?"

"Only when you didn't call after we came back to Paris. Fine if you want to keep things casual, but not if you expect to go incommunicado and only come around for booty calls."

He raised an eyebrow. "Classy."

"No, it's not. And that's why I don't want any part of something like that."

"I thought you might need space."

From anyone else, it might have seemed like a line, but she could feel the real sincerity in his voice. And she knew he was probably right. She really, probably did need space. Because their intimacy had been so complete in Malawi. He had been in her, and not just in a physical sense. She had shared everything with him. Had given him a piece of her.

And maybe space would keep her feeling from developing into something that was absolutely futile.

"Well, I don't. I mean, it would have been nice to be sure of where we stood when we came back here."

Blaise dropped a soft kiss on her lips and she froze, luxuriating in the feel of his mouth on hers. It really had been too long.

When they parted he stayed close to her, his voice low. "No matter what I intended, I think it's clear what our relationship has to be, as long as we're in close proximity."

Ella shivered. "I suppose so."

He let his fingers drift over her cheek, his eyes intent on hers. "I cannot seem to keep my hands off of you."

The crowd completely receded, the low hum of voices becoming nothing more than white noise. There was only Blaise, only his hand on her cheek, his gaze on her, full of a deep longing that echoed in her body.

She closed the distance between them, sliding her tongue delicately over the seam of his lips, tasting him, savoring him like a craving she'd been aching to partake of.

She placed her hands lightly on his chest, felt his heart raging against her palm. He gripped her wrist and pulled it back, stepped away from her.

"No," he said, his voice rough.

"Why not?"

"Business, remember?"

"Oh, right."

It probably wouldn't look very good for Blaise to be making out with her in the middle of the oh-so-upscale event. Especially since he had business to discuss.

"I promise to behave myself," she whispered.

He looked at her for a long moment, her skin burning beneath his close scrutiny. "Now, that is a shame."

Ella felt her body get hot everywhere, her breasts heavy. She longed for his hands to cup her there, to alleviate the ache of unsatisfied longing. Not here. Of course not here.

Blaise took Ella's hand and led her to the bar, to the purpose for his attendance. Calder Williams, owner of a very upscale chain of hotels, and the next project Blaise wanted to invest his money in.

Ella shifted next to him, her breast brushing his arm. All of his blood rushed south. His body was on fire with the need to be inside her again, to move his hands over her body, to be in her body. Two days had been more than enough time apart. It had been important to him to prove that he could conquer his need for her by staying away.

But he had proven that point, and he was done waiting. Business first, though, pleasure later.

"Calder," Blaise said, extending his hand, his mind back on business, even if his body was still stubbornly stuck on Ella.

"Blaise—" Calder accepted his hand "—good to see you again." His eyes were firmly fixed on Ella, the interest there obvious.

Blaise gritted his teeth. "Yes, it is."

"And you are?" Calder said to Ella.

"Ella Stanton." Ella extended her hand and Calder lifted it to his lips, brushing his mouth over Ella's creamy-soft skin.

Something ugly and dark kicked Blaise in the gut. The need to stake his claim, to show that Ella was his, blotted out everything else in his mind. He slid his arm around her waist, cupping her hip possessively, stroking her idly as he brought up his thoughts on Calder's hotel expansion project.

Calder's eyes continued to linger on Ella, his interest clearly on her curves not on business.

His dates had always been an accessory, in his mind, and if men had wanted to admire them, he had never cared. But he didn't want Calder looking at Ella. Didn't want him looking at her flawless face and luscious figure, and finding her desirable. Didn't want him looking at her scars and finding her lacking.

Ella was his.

"I think," Blaise said, his voice icy, "we should continue this discussion in my office another day."

A knowing smile curved Calder's lips. "I'll call your PA."

"Good."

"Nice to meet you, Ella," Calder said.

"You, too." Ella sounded unfazed, as though she had no idea that Calder had been contemplating having her for dessert. The thought made Blaise's blood run hot.

"Do you have a business card?" Calder asked.

Ella reached into her bright pink handbag and produced one. "Yes, this has all the info for the boutique and how to contact me personally for info about the clothing line."

"A fashion designer, I should have known."

"Calder, perhaps you should try preying on one of the single women in attendance and leave my date to me."

Ella stiffened beside him, Calder's grin widened. "Of course," he said, tucking Ella's business card into the interior pocket of his jacket.

"Nice to meet you," Ella said, gripping Blaise's arm. "I think I'm ready to go."

Ella released her hold on him once they got a few feet away from Calder, moving quickly to keep ahead of him, weaving through the crowd and heading toward the door.

Blaise followed her out into the empty corridor. "And what is your problem? I thought you wanted to come?"

"I didn't know you were going to spend the evening acting like a jealous jerk."

"Like you were earlier today?"

She gritted her teeth and let out a mild growl. "I didn't embarrass you in front of anyone."

"He was ready to devour you in front of me."

"But I wouldn't have allowed it, so what was the problem?"

"The problem is that this was meant to be a business meeting of sorts, and that was decidedly unprofessional."

"Don't blame me for your display of possessive male behavior, Blaise Chevalier."

Her blue eyes were on fire, all but spitting sparks at him, her cheeks red with her very indelicate rage. But his eyes went straight to her lips. Full, electric-pink thanks to her expertly applied gloss. Kissable. Edible. *Necessary.*

Ella had been a virgin less than a week ago. Out of deference to that, he shouldn't follow through with the fantasies rioting in his brain. But he couldn't stop himself.

There was a time in his life when he'd considered himself a man of honor. A man in control of his baser instincts.

All pretense of that had been well and truly destroyed three years ago, and he had destroyed it with his own hands. Tonight he would not be gaining those qualities back. He had to taste Ella. He *had* to. It was a matter far beyond simple attraction. It was elemental, bone deep and as necessary as breathing. To prove that she was his. That he was the man she wanted, not Calder, or any other. To ensure that no matter how many men brought her to pleasure after him, he would be the one she always remembered.

He captured her mouth. His body shuddering as her lips softened, parted for him immediately. He delved in, his tongue sliding over hers, his body instantly hard, instantly aching from the sweet pressure of her lips.

She kissed him back. Roughly. Passionately. Her hands moving up to bracket his face. He stepped forward and she moved with him until her back was against the wall. And he kept kissing her, like he was dying and this was the last moment he would ever have to seize the most essential experience before the end.

The kiss was fueled by desperation, a desperation he couldn't understand or control. It was coursing through him with an intensity that rocked him to the core, driving him on with an urgency he'd never experienced before. Maybe it was his anger, mixing with hers, creating a substance that was deadly and explosive.

This was no civil prelude to an evening of uncomplicated pleasure. This was something more. Something deeper. As it had been from the moment he'd first touched Ella.

"Blaise," she whispered.

"Ella." He met her eyes, kissed her cheek, her neck, right on the place where the fire had marked her skin. Then he moved to kiss the other side of her neck, leaving two kisses there, as he had promised to do.

She arched against him, and he put his hand between

them, palmed her breast, his thumb stroking over her hardened nipple.

She was everything he remembered and more. Her flavor richer, more intoxicating, the feeling of her against him more arousing than anything in his memory. The sounds of her pleasure, the movement of her body as she exulted in his touch, it was all so much more, and it all served to fray the edges of his tightly held control.

He moved his hand down, gripped her hips, pulled her hard against his body so she could feel the heavy length of his erection. So she would know exactly what she was doing to him.

A voluptuous sigh escaped her lips and she let her hands move down his back, gripping his butt, drawing his body even tighter into hers.

He was on the brink, in the corridor where anyone could see them, not even a convenient pillar to shield them from prying eyes, he was ready to come. When it came to sex, Blaise preferred a bedroom and privacy, but it didn't seem important now.

Nothing did. Nothing except his need to have Ella.

There was a sharp sound as the main doors to the ballroom opened and came into contact with the metal doorstop.

Ella froze, slowly releasing her hold on him. He moved away from her, but only fractionally, keeping one hand on her waist.

A small group of people wandered out, talking and laughing, visibly intoxicated and not paying any attention to Ella and himself.

Ella dropped her head, her forehead pressing against his shoulder after the group passed by. "Oh…that was…I don't know what just happened."

"Lust."

"Lust," she repeated. "Maybe that's it." But she didn't sound convinced. She didn't convince him.

Ella's eyes looked huge, her pupils dilated, her breasts rising and falling unevenly, along with her breathing.

"Your place or mine?" he asked, his voice strangled.

"I only have a single bed."

Another stark reminder of how innocent she was. Of what a bastard he was.

"Mine then."

CHAPTER TWELVE

BLAISE's apartment was a brilliant reflection of the man himself. Hard, cool, with smooth lines and nothing that betrayed a clue about his true inner workings.

Not a family photo. Not even artwork that went beyond generic, modern prints that Ella was certain an interior designer had selected for him.

It reflected what he showed the world, but it didn't reflect what she knew about him. Blaise was Malawi. The lake, the sky, the sense of beauty that hadn't been, and never could be, tamed.

But this, this slick, cool environment, was what he wanted the world to believe. Was what he was comfortable with.

"Lovely view," Ella said, gesturing to a wall of windows that revealed the Paris skyline, the brightly lit Eiffel tower glittering prominently.

Blaise shrugged, flickering the windows a disinterested glance. "I hardly notice it."

Ella nearly choked. "Then why...I mean, this didn't come cheap. Why have it if you don't appreciate the location?"

"Oh, I do appreciate the location. This penthouse was a good investment, because of the view, mainly."

She cleared her throat. "That's...well, it's very you."

"You have the soul of an artist, Ella," he said, his tone indulgent. "I have the soul of a financier. You see art, I see monetary value."

"That's your passion then, money?"

He shrugged again, discarding his coat carelessly on the couch and loosening his tie. "Not money itself. Making it. The challenge, the risk."

"So, you're a gambler?"

"Hardly. My risks are all very carefully calculated. I don't take chances."

"You don't consider your association with me taking a chance?"

"*Non.* You have talent, Ella. It has been confirmed by everyone I've spoken to on the subject."

Ella took a deep breath, continuing to survey the vast, empty feeling space. Everything was so unnaturally clean, so strangely organized.

"I'm not home very often," Blaise said, answering some of the questions that were rattling around in her head.

"Ah."

Blaise crossed the room, his eyes intent on her, and the sterile background faded away.

The moment his lips met hers, the fire was reignited in him, and he was consumed by it. Consumed by his need to have her. It had never been like this before. Not with any woman, not in any fantasy.

It managed to reach in past the walls he'd built inside himself, managed to make him feel the full force of his need, the full force of his arousal, without the protective shield that he prized so much.

And he didn't want to stop her. Didn't want to do

anything that might dampen any part of what she made him feel.

Her hands went to his chest, fingers working the buttons of his shirt without any finesse. She made a small sound of frustration when she stumbled at one of the buttons, and he laughed, finished the job for her and consigning his shirt to the floor.

"You're perfect," she whispered, her hand skimming his bare chest.

His heart squeezed tight. She meant his body, because if she could see inside him, she would know what a lie that statement was. Would know just how far from perfect he was.

"My bedroom is upstairs," he said, moving it all into safer territory. To bed. He could give her everything there. All of his desire, all of the pleasure that was possible for her to have.

It was the only place he could give her everything she deserved.

She smiled wickedly, parting from him and sauntering up the curved staircase that led to his room. Her backside swayed back and forth in an enticing rhythm and he was powerless to look anywhere else.

His room had the same view as the living area, the Paris skyline, the *Tour Eiffel*. A view that represented nothing to him. Nothing but broken promises. Marie's and his own. It was a view he had purchased at Marie's command.

The view was all that remained the same. After she'd left, gone off with the new love of her life, he'd brought in a decorator to eradicate the feminine frills his ex had brought into the penthouse. He had made a valiant effort to erase every reminder of her. What he hadn't been about to do was sell a valuable piece of real estate at a bad time, not even when he was—or so he'd believed then—heartbroken.

So he'd spent three years ignoring the view. But now, when he looked out his windows, he would see Ella's silhouette in the foreground, the lights glittering behind her, as he did now. She was looking at him with stark longing on her face, none of the coyness some of his other lovers liked to employ.

Ella wanted him, and she did not bother to hide it. Her honesty was stunning, more than he deserved. And yet he wanted it. Wanted her. All of her.

She looked behind her, at the open windows.

"It is privacy glass. Even with the lights on, no one can see in," he said.

Ella nodded, reaching behind her back. "Good. Because tonight—" he heard the rasp of her zipper "—I want the lights on."

He could see she was nervous, could see the slight tremor in her hand as she eased her sheath dress down her body, shimmying to release it over the curve of her hips.

His body hardened to the point of pain at the sight of her, her gorgeous curves on display, barely covered by a nearly sheer bra and panty set. This was the first time, during a sexual encounter, that she had revealed her body to him in full light.

Ella Stanton was the bravest woman he had ever met. A combination of softness and strength, insecurity and confidence. A woman who had endured such pain with no support.

She threw the vapid nature of his life, of the lives of the people he associated with, into sharp relief.

His mind went clear of everything but the sight of her as she unhooked her bra and revealed her breasts. Soft and pale, light pink tips that looked like the sweetest treats. Treats he couldn't resist.

He moved to her, brushing his fingers lightly over her collarbone, down around the outside curve of her breast to her ribs. She whimpered slightly and he repeated the motion, not touching her where he knew she longed for it.

His own body pulsed in protest. He didn't want slow. He wanted now. He wanted immediate satisfaction. He also wanted to savor her. To give her everything he had to give. This was it for him, the beginning and the end of what he had for her.

It wasn't enough.

She wiggled against him, tugging her panties down and kicking them to the side, along with her spiky heels.

He reached between them, rubbing his fingers over the intimate heart of her body, dipping one finger into her, drawing out her moisture and slicking it over her clitoris. He did it again. Again, until she was weak in his arms, desperate sounds of pleasure escaping her lips.

He pushed another finger into her, searching for the point inside of her body that would bring her to the heights faster. He continued moving his thumb over the bundle of nerves at the apex of her thighs.

She clung to his shoulders, and he welcomed the bite of her nails, the pain distracting him from the force of his arousal, helping him hold on when he was so close to slipping over the edge into oblivion without giving her satisfaction.

"Blaise, I can't…" she panted.

"Come for me," he said roughly, driven to feel her climax around his fingers, to experience her pleasure that way.

She bit her lip, pink color flooding over her skin, spreading across her cheeks, down over her breasts. When her orgasm hit, she shuddered against him, her body trembling, growing heavier as she rested her weight on him.

"Ma belle," he whispered, scooping her into his arms and carrying her to the bed. He gently placed her in the middle, working at discarding the rest of his clothes before joining her.

She took his erection in her hand, her eyes locked with his as she squeezed him, pleasured him. This was no practiced move performed for hundreds of others; this was simply for him. He owed her the same.

He pressed his lips to her neck, nibbled the delicate skin there before moving on to her breasts. "You are like a dessert," he said, running the tip of his tongue around the outside of one hardened nipple. "Strawberries and cream. But much better, much richer."

He sucked the tightened bud between his lips and she arched against him, abandoning her attentions on his body, her focus solely on her own satisfaction. As it should be. As he wanted it to be.

"I want you, Blaise," she said, her fingers skimming over his biceps, his shoulders, his back. "Only you."

His body pulsed with the need to be inside her, the need to take her, but he held onto the last shred of his control, moved his attention to her other breast.

"Please," she said. "Now."

His control shattered, all thoughts of drawing things out, of bringing her to peak after peak, dissolved. His mind was blank of everything but his need, his need to be in her, to be sheathed in her tight body.

Ella's body.

With shaking fingers he took a condom from his side

table drawer and ripped open the packaging. Ella held out her hand. "Let me."

"No," he ground out. "If you touch me, I'm going to come."

"I don't mind," she said, a wicked smile playing over her lips.

"Not like this, Ella."

"Yes," she said, taking the packet from his hand and setting it on the bed. "Like this."

She leaned forward, running her tongue over the length of him. His stomach seized tight, every muscle in his body locked, frozen, as she explored him with her mouth, her lips, her tongue.

She cupped him, took him deep into her mouth. The feeling of her tongue on him so intense he nearly lost it. He speared his fingers through her hair, planning to protest, to stop her, unable to bring himself to do it.

When she pressed a hot kiss to him he jerked away.

"Ella," he said. "I can't…"

She looked at him, her blue eyes hot. "Come for me, Blaise."

She turned her attention back to his body, back to his pleasure, taking very little effort to bring him past the point of no return and push him over the edge. He was no longer in control. She had taken it from him.

In a graceful movement, she came to rest beside him, her hand on his chest, her cheek on his shoulder.

"I love the contrast of your skin against mine," she said, her voice muffled.

"You do?"

"Yes. It's like art."

"As I said, you have the soul of an artist." And the lips of an enchantress.

She sighed, a soft sound, filled with emotion he couldn't guess at. "I'm sort of exhausted," she said.

"You are?" If anyone should be exhausted, it was him.

She smiled at him, a smile that didn't quite reach her eyes. "Very."

He'd never been in tune with the feelings of his lovers, he'd been told that very thing by several of them, but he knew that something was wrong with Ella. Sensed some kind of deep sadness in her. Felt it echo in his chest.

He shouldn't be surprised. It was all he'd ever given to those in his life that meant the most to him.

Ella's eyes fluttered closed, her breathing becoming deep and even. Blaise laid his head back on the pillow, his eyes wide-open. Sleep wouldn't be coming for him tonight.

Ella's entire body ached. In the early hours of the morning, Blaise had finished what they'd started, taking her to heights she hadn't imagined possible. Showing her things about herself she hadn't realized.

Ella rolled over in bed, her hand coming to rest on the cold spot where Blaise had been. She blew out a breath.

She didn't know how it happened, when it had happened, but at some point last night, after she'd lost her patience with his slow, controlled seduction and she'd taken it upon herself to shatter his control, as he'd shattered hers, she realized that she loved him.

She was in love with Blaise Chevalier. Notorious womanizer, the man who had stolen his brother's fiancée, the man who had commandeered her business loan like the pirate that the press said he was.

In her mind, she knew he was all of those things.

Every word they've printed about me is true. He'd said it. He'd meant it. But she didn't see it in him.

He was the man who traced her scars. The man who had held her while she'd told him all of her darkest secrets, tears streaming down her face. The man who believed in her talent, her visions. The man who thought she was beautiful.

He hardly seemed like he could be the same man the press wrote about. The man the people of France loved to hate.

The question was, what did it mean for her?

She'd known his darkest secrets from day one. But it hadn't stopped her from falling in love with him. Couldn't stop her. He was a bad bet, no question. Falling in love with him was akin to begging for heartbreak, and yet…she wasn't afraid, or sad, that she loved him.

Because last night, she had felt like a whole woman. A whole person. Someone who could be with the man she loved, do whatever she pleased, with the man she loved. There was nothing holding her back, no voice telling her she wasn't good enough or pretty enough.

Her effect on Blaise was obvious. He wasn't lying about his attraction to her. And that a man like him, a man who epitomized masculine perfection, could find her beautiful was something that made her rethink everything she'd ever thought about herself.

She wasn't in the waiting room of her own life anymore. She was living it. And she was very likely going to get her heart broken. But she wasn't hiding anymore.

Blaise came back into the bedroom, a towel wrapped around his waist, water droplets running down his impressive chest. She just wanted to lick them off. She was seriously starting to wonder if she was insatiable.

"Tell me about Marie," she said, the words slipping

out of her mouth before she had a chance to think them through.

He froze for a moment, then undid the towel and let it drop before moving over to the large, dark armoire in the corner of the bedroom, totally unconcerned with his nudity. "Why?"

"Because. Shouldn't I know?"

She saw his jaw tighten, a fractional movement that someone less in tune with him would have missed. "Look it up on the internet."

Her stomach tightened. "I have."

"Was that not enough?"

"No. It's not even close to being enough."

"It doesn't matter, Ella."

"Yes, Blaise, it matters."

"Why do you say that?" he asked, rolling his powerful shoulders as if trying to ease off stress. As if she was causing him stress.

"Because if it wasn't a big deal you would tell me about her."

He opened the top drawer to the armoire and took out a pair of black boxer briefs. He put them on, his body backlit by the sun filtering through the window.

"She was engaged to Luc. About three weeks before the wedding, she and I were alone at their penthouse. I seduced her. She called off the wedding. We had one year together, and then she left me."

Ella blinked, drawing her knees up to her chest. "I thought...I thought you broke up with her."

"No," he said, clipped.

"But you said every word written about you was true."

"More or less. The important parts are true. And I may as well have ended things. I drove her away. I wasn't very much fun to be around, since I looked at her and saw the betrayal of my brother."

"Why did you…why?"

"Why?" he repeated. "Because I loved her, you know. At least that was my excuse. Love conquers all, yes? Even an engagement ring."

"You loved her?" A sharp tug of jealousy pulled at Ella. He had loved Marie enough to do anything to have her. She'd assumed, all this time, that he'd seduced her, maybe to get revenge on the brother who'd been raised in luxury while he'd been in Africa with his mother.

But love…she hadn't considered that. Her pirate, with all those walls around his heart, had been open with someone else. Had given his heart to someone else. Believing that he had been callous in his seduction of Marie had almost been easier.

"No. I did not love her. I believed it was love, and what a convenient excuse it makes, *non?* An excuse to be selfish, an excuse to have big, screaming fights, because love is so passionate and the heart wants what it wants. The heart is a wicked thing, Ella."

"I don't believe that."

"Because you have not seen it. Have not seen how far it can lead you from everything you believed you were. I prefer to use my mind now. That, I can trust." He looked out the window. "Do you know why I have this view? Because of her. She begged for a view of the Eiffel Tower, such status, and how wonderful for when she threw parties. One of the many things I did to prove my love for her, an easy way to prove it, because all I had to do was write a check. Tell me, Ella, is that love?"

"No."

"I thought not."

Ella's stomach was tight. Jealousy, sadness, anger, all

rolled through her. She got out of the bed, not caring about her state of undress. Not even caring about her scars.

When she'd told Blaise about her family, she'd felt like a bond had been forged between them. She'd thought learning about his past would make it even stronger. But now she felt as if he'd just moved further away from him. As if the tenuous bond between them was fraying.

"I have to go to work," she said, stiffly. "I'll just… go home and use the shower there. I need new clothes anyway."

Blaise shrugged, tugging on a pair of dark blue jeans. "Have you heard back from Statham's?"

Ella shook her head. "Not yet."

"Let me know?"

Ella nodded, her heart feeling like it might be breaking in her chest. "Yeah. I'll call you."

CHAPTER THIRTEEN

"Hi," Ella said, stepping into Blaise's office. The view from there was just as spectacular as the view from his apartment. The thought made her stomach clench tight. She hadn't spoken to Blaise in twenty-four hours. Not since she'd left his penthouse after his revelation about Marie. And that was what the view reminded her of, the penthouse he'd bought for the woman he'd loved.

"What's your news, Ella?" he asked, his gaze barely flickering away from his computer screen.

"I just got a slot in a really big fashion show coming up next week," Ella said.

"Great," Blaise said, though he didn't sound shocked. "How did that come about."

"There was a cancellation, and the organizers of the event called me. It's going to cost a bit to throw together so last minute, but I can show the line that Statham's is looking at, my collection for Fall of next year."

"You have models?"

"I have most of them. I suppose we could trawl your black book if I need any more."

That got his attention, a wry smile curving his lips. "If you need it, it's in the vault at my bank."

"I'm sure it contains State secrets," she said, smiling back in spite of herself.

"Possible incriminating evidence. Though I'm not sure much more could be done to damage my reputation."

Not likely. His reputation was well and truly damaged, and he seemed to revel in that. Seemed to wear it like a comfortable coat. She couldn't figure out why. And she wanted to, so badly. She wanted to know his heart, the heart that he saw as being so wicked. She wanted to know *him*.

"Probably not," she said, her throat tight. "You didn't…did you arrange for this?"

"No, Ella. I didn't arrange for Statham's to contact you, either."

A little bubble of satisfaction expanded in her chest. She'd appreciated Blaise's help so much along the way, but to know she'd done it on her own was huge. Because someday, she would be managing without Blaise entirely, both professionally and personally. She had to know she could do this alone. And the good thing was, now, she was sure that she could.

She didn't want to, but she could.

It was funny that not so long ago she'd been dreaming of the day she could pay him off as quickly as possible and get him out of her life. Now she didn't want to lose him. It would be funny if she didn't know it would hurt so bad when he walked out of her life. And he would. Because if he didn't love her, what would hold him to her? His sexual fascination with her would fade. It had to.

Although, she doubted the fascination she had for him would ever fade. Even now her body ached for him. Almost as much as her heart.

"I just wanted to tell you," she said. And she wanted to hug him. And kiss him. And tell him that she loved him.

"I'm proud of you, Ella."

Her heart stalled. It was the first time she could remember someone saying that to her, and it couldn't have meant more coming from anyone else.

"Thank you. I'd better go make some phone calls."

Blaise stood from his desk and crossed to her, putting his arms around her waist. He dipped his head and kissed her, his lips hot on hers, familiar and foreign at the same time.

"I'll see you tonight," he said.

She nodded. "Okay." It might be emotional suicide, but she was willing to take the chance.

Because some things were worth taking a chance on. Blaise was one of them.

The next week passed in a haze. Work filled up her day and Blaise took up each and every night, the passion between them only growing stronger each time they were together.

Ella's feelings for him growing stronger.

The night of the fashion show was chaotic, the backstage a blur of half-dressed models and screaming stage managers. Ella loved it. She was in her element. And tonight her confidence wasn't a show.

The woman she pretended to be had finally melded with the woman she was. She wasn't quite as outrageous as her persona had been, but she wasn't crippled by insecurity, either. She was happy now. Her makeup wasn't a mask, her clothes weren't armor. She was just Ella. And she was happy with that. And she was enough.

The voice in her head was Blaise now, telling her that she was beautiful, that she had talent. She wasn't bogged down by doubt anymore. She wasn't living in the tragedy that had happened eleven years earlier.

Ella watched on the monitor backstage as her line

was paraded out in front of the audience. Listened to the applause. And, when it was time for Ella to walk out with her model wearing the finale piece, and she grabbed the other woman's hand and did her turn on the catwalk, confidence surged through her.

When she reached the backstage it was still in complete chaos. Another designer's work was going on in ten minutes and models and stylists were scrambling here and there in an attempt to get everything done on time.

Ella turned and saw Sarah Chadwick, the head buyer for Statham's, making her way through the throng of people. "Ella, that was fabulous."

"Thank you. I'm so glad I was able to participate."

"I'm glad you did, too. I think you make the kind of clothing that I want to see in Statham's. It's wearable, but it has an edge that I love."

"You want my line in your stores?" Ella knew she sounded a little bit breathless and shocked, but she was.

"I do. And I'm sure I won't be the only one. But if you can get us some exclusive pieces, I'm sure I can sweeten up the contract."

"I can…I can do that."

"I'll be sending over the paperwork later in the week and I…" Sarah checked the monitor behind them. "I'd better get back out there and watch the rest of this show. I'll be in touch."

Ella just stood there, letting the activity move around her. Statham's had been such a huge goal for her. To have achieved it was almost surreal. And the first person she wanted to share the news with was Blaise. He was the one who'd helped her get to this point, he was the one who'd really made it possible.

And he was the most important person in her life.

She turned and saw him, standing apart from the crowd of people. He was dressed in the suit from her line that she'd fitted to him, and he was holding a pink rose. The crowd faded away and she could picture him standing by a lake in Malawi, rose in hand. The night he'd traced her scars.

She walked over to him, her heart pounding in her chest. "I'm glad you're here."

"Well done," he said, handing her the rose. She touched it lightly, the texture of the velvet petals weaving sensual memories around her.

"I got the contract with Statham's. I just spoke to the head buyer."

He nodded slightly. "I knew you would."

"Only because you're too arrogant to admit otherwise."

He shrugged. "Or I have great confidence in you."

"I'll choose to believe that."

"When can you leave?" he asked, sensual intent threaded through his rich voice.

"I can leave now," she said. Because everything had been wonderful, and she'd just experienced a career high, and all she wanted to do was celebrate it with the man she loved.

"It's beautiful, Blaise." Blaise watched Ella's face as she surveyed the apartment. Candles were resting on every flat surface in the bedroom, except for the bed, casting a warm glow on everything the light touched.

"You don't mind candles?" He wondered if the fire might bother her.

She shook her head. "They're gorgeous. As long as we blow them out when we're done."

"Of course."

No, they wouldn't bother his Ella. She didn't hold on to her fear.

"Thank you. This is special. Tonight was special."

It had been. Watching Ella's clothes on the catwalk, seeing her come out and join the models, waving and smiling, taking ownership of her work, had made him feel like his chest was expanding.

And now, seeing her like this, bathed in the dim light, he felt as though he might explode with wanting her. With his desire to see her come to the peak of pleasure at his hands, but more than that, the desire to make her happy. To make her feel as special as she was.

"Come here, Ella."

Her blue eyes glittered with mischief in the flickering candlelight. "You come here, Mr. Chevalier."

And he did, because he was powerless to refuse her.

His blood ran hot and fast through his body, a fire raging out of control. He looked at Ella's body, skimmed his fingertips down the scar on her neck. That was the damage left by fire.

He tried to turn on his practiced seducer persona. He was a pro at it. He knew how to reduce a woman to a mass of quivering need while keeping his own desires in check, not taking his pleasure until the very last moment, after she had reached the peak several times.

But there was too much urgency in him, too much need. His body throbbed with it, his brain closed off to everything but the feel of her silken skin beneath his fingertips, everything but the ache in his hardened erection. Everything but the driving need to be in her. To make her his.

His woman. His Ella.

Ella did the seducing, her hands, her lips, her tongue. His muscles shook with the effort of keeping himself from falling over the edge.

She was beautiful like this. Wild. Abandoned. Confident. Allowing her body to be bathed in firelight, unashamed, unafraid.

"Let me have you, Blaise," she whispered as he laid her back on the bed. "All of you."

The need in her voice, the desperation, pushed him past the point of return. If Ella hadn't placed the condom in his hand, he would have forgotten. Never, in all his life, had he forgotten about protection. He rolled it on with unsteady hands and thrust into her body, teeth clenched tight as pleasure poured over him like warm oil.

His mind was blank. Desire clouding everything, blocking out his usual reserve, his slow, practiced rhythm. All he could do was chase his satisfaction.

Ella arched against him, her tight nipples brushing against his chest. She gripped his butt, her fingers digging into his skin, soft, smooth legs locked around his calves as she moved against him, an active participant, as wild and out of control as he was.

"Blaise," she said hoarsely, her internal muscles clenching around him, pulling his own response from him.

He let out a harsh groan as he came, his body trembling in the aftermath of the intense release.

He rolled to the side, bringing Ella with him, his brain in a fog, his entire body heavy. Satisfied in a way he never had been before, and at the same time, hungry for more of her. He would always be hungry for more of her.

He was losing his control, could feel it slipping from

his hands even now, the walls inside of him crumbling, leaving him exposed, allowing him to feel. He took a breath, and her scent filled him. His heart clenched tight.

It was unacceptable. He could not allow it.

Ella felt like she was walking on a cloud. The fashion show had been a success, her clothing line would be featured in one of the world's largest upscale department stores and she'd spent the entire night making love with Blaise.

Blaise. The man she loved.

She smiled as she pinned the sleeves on the jacket she was working on. She'd had to send some of her patterns out to sample makers since the workload was increasing, but there were a few key pieces she wanted to make sure she had a hand in, and her pink and gray trench was one of them.

The door to her studio opened and Ella turned sharply as Blaise strode in, his expression blank, his jaw tight. "You should lock the door," he said, his voice low.

"Sorry," she said, her stomach clenching. Everything about Blaise's body language spoke of intent, not of a casual visit. After last night, after the past week, she expected him to greet her with a kiss, not to stand with five feet of blank space between them, arms crossed.

"We have something we need to discuss."

Her stomach dropped. "Oh." It wasn't like she hadn't known it would happen eventually, wasn't as though she hadn't realized that a man who didn't believe in love wouldn't believe in commitment...but just because a prisoner knew the execution date was coming, didn't make it easier to bear.

And she'd thought...she'd thought it had changed. His

walls had been coming down. He didn't treat her like an anonymous sex object; he treated her like a prize. Surely that meant something. She didn't say that, though. She didn't say anything. She couldn't.

"I'm ending our business association," he said tightly, handing her a stack of tightly folded documents.

She took them, fingers numb at the tips as she tried to grasp them. She was certain he could see her shaking.

"But…my business…my…I have contracts. The Ella Stanton label is poised on the brink of making it, *I'm* poised on the brink of making it."

"I am not calling the loan in. I am gifting you the amount of the loan, and the amount of the investment."

Ella shook her head. "I don't…I don't understand. Is it because we're in a relationship? Because that doesn't make it feel right, either. I can't just take money from you."

"You didn't seem to mind taking favors from me, connections, but if you've suddenly become above that, don't worry. We will end our personal association as well," he said, his voice flat, echoing in the expanse of the room.

She felt like the walls were closing in on her. "Why?"

"I've told you why. In truth I'm shocked you didn't end things when I told you about Marie. So now, I will do it for you."

"Why is that, Blaise?" she asked, her voice low, anger surging through her. "Because you couldn't chase me away with the revelation of what a bad, bad man you are? And now you have to do it by being more direct? Because you were counting on that to get rid of me weren't you? Counting on your reputation to chase me away."

"It would get rid of anyone sane," he said, flatly.

"And this would, too? Right? This act you're pulling now, you standing there cold and flat when we both know how passionate you are." She could see it for what it was, she could see through him, and even though his words hurt, she knew they weren't real. She knew he was trying to protect himself. Because last night had cut deep, had forged a bond between them that was nearly frightening to her in intensity.

"I love you," she said. Why keep it a secret? Why lie when it was a truth that coursed through her veins, a truth that was in her, a part of her. Just like Blaise was a part of her.

He looked as though she'd struck him. "Stop."

"No. I can't. I won't."

"It's the sex, that's all. You were a virgin when we first made love and you're confusing lust with love. An easy thing to do, I know."

"Yes, yes, I was a virgin, thanks for the reminder. I also know that if this were only sex, the rumors of your reputation might have kept me at a distance. If it were only about sex then I would never have asked you about Marie. My heart wouldn't have bled for you, for the pain she put you through."

"The pain she put me through? It was a pain we brought on each other. One we both deserved."

"A pain you think you still deserve?"

He spoke through gritted teeth. "You don't know what you want. You don't want me, not for anything more than some fun in bed, trust me on that. I have nothing else for you."

"I do know what I want, Blaise. And I'm not going to

be talked down to, and told that I don't. You can blame yourself for that. You're the one who helped me find my strength, who helped me see that I was taking half when I deserved whole just like everyone else. And now, you're the one that's confused. You're the one that's afraid. It's so much easier for you to hold on to all of the stuff from the past because then you don't have to try, you don't have to take a risk. You don't have to put yourself out there again and take a chance on being wrong."

Blaise tightened his jaw, his eyes flat, void of emotion. A trick. One she'd seen him use before when she got too close, when he was feeling intensely.

"Are you really going to define your entire life by one mistake?" she asked.

When he spoke, his voice was low and hard. He didn't yell; he didn't need to. "That one mistake showed who I truly was. I thought I was such a great man, I had everything. A family that I was forging a new bond with. Position, power, wealth and honor. But none of it could stand up to my weakness," he said, his voice strained. "All the good I have done means nothing if I fail when it matters most."

Anger rose in her, along with desperation. Desperation to make him see himself. Really see himself, like she did. "Is that what bothers you most, Blaise Chevalier? The discovery that you're a man and not a god? That you're human, like everyone else? Well, I'm glad that you are. Because I needed a man to show me what I was missing. I needed a man to make me feel beautiful. I didn't need perfection. I needed someone who could understand *me*." She put her palm flat against her chest. "And you did. You were there for me. You've made me see. You've made me see everything I deserve. Everything I spent the past eleven years denying myself out of fear. I'm not afraid now. And it's because of you."

"You're wrong, Ella," he said, his voice hard, unsteady. "Because you seem to think if you keep digging you'll find some hidden depth to me, but the truth is, this is it. I have nothing more for you. I have nothing more for anyone."

Images flashed through Ella's mind. The yacht. The rose. The night she'd taken him into her mouth and he'd trembled with ecstasy.

"You're wrong," she said. "You're afraid, and also wrong. There is so much to you, Blaise Chevalier. You're selling yourself short, you're selling both of us short."

"And you've bought into a fantasy, Ella Stanton. But a fantasy is just that. Fantasy. Nothing." A muscle in his jaw ticked and for a moment she saw a flash of blinding pain in his golden eyes, pain that ripped into her, echoed through her body. "There is no reason for you to see me again."

He turned and walked out of the room, closing the door behind him with a slam that was painful in its finality.

Ella set the papers down on the table, the words across the top blurring as her eyes filled with tears. She gripped the edge of the table, so hard that it bit into her palms, and felt her heart splinter, shatter, the pieces falling and blowing away. Out the door with Blaise.

He had her heart forever, and she knew she would never get it back.

CHAPTER FOURTEEN

BLAISE gazed out the window of his penthouse, out at the view. The view he normally ignored. If he closed his eyes, he saw Ella, the bright lights of the city behind her, the silhouette of her curves much more enticing than any feat of man-made architecture.

He slammed his tumbler down onto the bar, whiskey sloshing over the side. When Marie had left, he'd gotten drunk. He'd called the last woman he'd dated and he'd lost himself in her body, using her to forget.

The thought of doing the same now made his stomach curdle, made him feel on the verge of physical sickness. He didn't want to forget Ella, he didn't want to touch another woman. He wanted to keep her essence on his skin, keep the feelings that he had for her at the surface. Even if all he had left was pain, he wanted to hold on to it.

Because there were feelings. Last night she'd torn down every defense he had, left him open and raw and bleeding.

He'd looked at her and seen everything she was. All of her heart and bravery. And he'd looked within himself and seen nothing. He wasn't afraid of heartbreak. He was experiencing it now in a way he'd never fathomed.

As though a hole had been punched through his chest, leaving a bloody chasm where his heart had been.

He wanted to crumble from the pain. Even as the thought passed his mind, he found himself going to his knees, still staring out the window. He had thought he'd known love, and he'd been wrong, he'd realized that years ago.

What he hadn't realized was that love was very real, and that the power it possessed was much more than he could have ever fathomed.

You're wrong. And you're scared.

Damn right.

But the fear of a broken heart was nothing compared to the fear of Ella one day realizing she deserved more than him. To look in her eyes and see the disillusionment and pain he'd seen in his brother's eyes the day he'd found out about his betrayal.

To see the fire in Ella's eyes dim. To see the love there turn to hate, that was what he couldn't face.

He had always counted on his control to shield him from pain, to keep a buffer between himself and others. Playing the bastard was fine, because it meant no one looked inside him. He was afraid that if they did, the truth would be that he was nothing more than a bastard. Hadn't he proven it with Marie? Hadn't he proven it by betraying the brother who had welcomed him in France with open arms?

Ella made him want to try to be more. He didn't know if his best could ever be good enough.

He stood, pressed his palm flat against the cold glass. It would have to be good enough. Because he could not live without her.

"Ella."

Two weeks without Blaise and now she was hallucinating. She'd dreamed his voice so many times that she was hearing it while she was awake now. She was in a hurry to get out of the gray, Parisian weather, and she really wasn't in the mood to experience more time in her own personal hell.

Life without Blaise. A reality she had accepted, but a reality that hurt like an open, never-healing wound every day. She rested her head against the door of her studio, hand frozen on the key that she had jammed into the lock.

The touch on her neck was soft, familiar, as her hair was brushed back. It made her ache. The soft brush of lips on the scarred side of her neck. And she knew if she angled so he could reach the other side he would kiss her twice there.

She turned her head and saw him standing there in the rain, shirt collar open, no tie. He looked like a mess. Cheekbones too prominent, deep shadows beneath his eyes, black stubble on his face. And she'd never seen a more wonderful sight in her life. Or a more painful one.

"Why are you here?" she whispered, her voice thick with tears. "You said I wouldn't have to see you again."

He looked down, as though he couldn't meet her eyes. A first. "If you do not wish to see me, I will go."

"Why are you here?" she asked. Because she did wish to see him, no matter how cruel the pain, she wanted to see him for as long as she could, to drink in the sight of him, to feel the warmth of his caress. To just be with him.

"Ella," he said again, his voice gruff.

Her first instinct was to throw her arms around him

and kiss him like she was love-starved. But she couldn't. Not until she knew why he was here.

If only she were love-starved, it might be better. Instead she was filled with it. It colored everything she did, everything she saw. She would put on a dress and actually feel beautiful, and think of him, think of all that he had done to build that confidence within her. She would hear a joke and want to tell Blaise, would taste a new flavor of ice cream and want to share it with him. Alone in her bed at night, her body ached, and there was no relief. Because there was no Blaise.

Because he wasn't with her. Because he didn't love her.

"I could not stay away," he said, his voice rough. "Every night, sleep evades me. Every day my body aches, and I cannot eat. You…you are vital to me, and I did not realize it until I chased you away."

He took her hand in his, traced the scarring on the back of it with his thumb. "You were right about me, Ella. I was afraid. I am afraid. I said I was never nervous, but I am, shaking to my core, terrified that I have destroyed this thing between us. I have been a fool."

Rain was still falling, water spots darkening his white dress shirt. He didn't seem to care. Neither did she. The streets could flood and she wouldn't be tempted to move. Nothing could entice her away from Blaise, now or ever.

"You told me," he said, his thumb still moving over her scar-roughened skin, "that I was perfect once. That my body was perfect, and all that time, you saw yourself as damaged when you were more whole than I could have hoped to be."

She bit her lip and shook her head. "That's where you're wrong. I wasn't whole, I was fragmented, scared.

That's how I recognized that fear in you, because I lived with it for so long. You helped me overcome it. You helped me realize that I was just sitting back waiting to live life when…I had nothing to wait for. You woke me up."

He kissed her then and her heart expanded. He wasn't here for work. He wasn't even here to tell her about his family. He was here for her. She kissed him back, slick lips sliding together in the pouring rain. Her skin was cold, but Blaise's hands warmed her, his lips on her neck lit a trail of fire that burned through her.

But this fire was different. It cleansed where it touched, burned away all of the debris that life had left both of them, so that there was nothing but Blaise and Ella.

"You've changed me," he said when they parted.

He traced the marks on her neck, reverently, his eyes never leaving hers. "I was afraid that if you ever saw past the walls I had put up, you would see nothing but a barren wasteland. I was afraid I could give you nothing."

"You've given me everything," she whispered. "You might not see it, Blaise, but you have. I was locked in myself, my body was my prison. And you set me free. When I look in you I see the world. Everything I've ever wanted or could ever want."

"I stand before you with no walls," he said, brushing his thumb over her lips, "I am not perfect, but I am a man who loves you very much, and I will do everything in my power to be all you deserve."

Everything in her expanded, filled, all of the love she had for him growing, rushing through her veins. "I didn't think you believed in love," she said, a smile on her face she could not hold back.

He pressed his forehead against hers, a smile curving his lips. "It was so much easier to believe that. Because as long as I believed everything had been a lie, I could pretend that I would never falter in that way again."

He took her hands in his, brought them to his lips. "I was wrong, again. Love is very real, Ella Stanton, and I know it because I love you with every fiber of my being. It's more than simple passion, more than lust. It is nothing I've ever known before. It's in every part of me. You are in me. The best parts of me. It isn't a facade for lust or selfishness, how can it be? If it were only my body that needed you, my heart wouldn't hurt every time it beat without you. If it were selfishness, you wouldn't have given me so much."

Tears were sliding down Ella's cheeks, mixing with the rain. And she didn't care. She didn't bother to wipe them away.

"I love you, too. I didn't even need you to do anything, to change. I just love you. All that you are, all that you've been, everything you will be."

Blaise's heart beat fast in his chest, without pain for the first time in two weeks, as Ella said the words that he had thrown aside that day at her studio. Words he'd been sure he would never hear from her lips again. Words he knew he'd done nothing to earn or deserve.

"I did need to change, Ella. You have changed me. You talked of being locked inside of yourself, and I had done that same thing, hiding behind my defenses. Defenses you wouldn't allow me to keep. You demand so much of me."

She nodded her head, blond curls swinging, flicking rainwater. "Because I needed all of you."

"You have all of me. I swear it. I will never hide from

you again. And you will have my love, my body, my heart, for the rest of my days."

"How do you know that?" she asked, the tears clouding her brilliant blue eyes.

"Because being without you, losing you, was the lowest point of my life. There is nothing that comes close to rivaling it."

"Same goes for me," she said. "Never put either of us through that again."

"I won't." He reached into his pocket and pulled out a small velvet box. It was the ring he'd bought the night after he'd gone to his knees in his penthouse. Because he'd known that he had to have her back, that he had to do this. That he would lay down every shred of pride left and get on his knees before her if he had to, to try to convince her to take him back. To try to convince her to be with him forever.

Pride was nothing in the face of losing Ella. There was no room for it, not if it stood in the way of this.

"Be with me," he said, lowering himself to his knee. "Always. Be my wife."

She knelt down in front of him, the knees of her designer jeans on the wet sidewalk. She put her hand on his cheek, her eyes never leaving his. "Always."

He opened the box and delighted in the look on her face. "It's pink," she said, pulling the round cut, platinum-set bubblegum-pink diamond ring from its box.

"It's you." He slid it onto her finger, over the roughened patches that had been touched by fire. A hand uniquely Ella's and completely perfect in his eyes.

"It is," she said. "You know me so well."

"And you know me, and seem to love me anyway."

She leaned into him, her hands bracketing his face. "I love you because I know you."

He kissed her. He would never have enough of her lips. He would never have enough of her. He slid his hands beneath her shirt, felt the landscape of her skin. Felt the story of who she was with his fingertips.

"You are absolutely perfect, Ella Chevalier. In every way."

* * * * *

A sneaky peek at next month...

MODERN™

INTERNATIONAL AFFAIRS, SEDUCTION & PASSION GUARANTEED

My wish list for next month's titles...

In stores from 19th August 2011:

- ❏ The Kanellis Scandal — Michelle Reid
- ❏ One Night in the Orient — Robyn Donald
- ❏ The Sultan's Choice — Abby Green
- ❏ Girl in the Bedouin Tent — Annie West
- ❏ Revealed: His Secret Child — Sandra Hyatt

In stores from 2nd September 2011:

- ❏ Monarch of the Sands — Sharon Kendrick
- ❏ His Poor Little Rich Girl — Melanie Milburne
- ❏ The Return of the Stranger — Kate Walker
- ❏ Once Touched, Never Forgotten — Natasha Tate

Available at WHSmith, Tesco, Asda, Eason, Amazon and Apple

Just can't wait?

Visit us Online

You can buy our books online a month before they hit the shops! **www.millsandboon.co.uk**

0811/

2 Free Books!

Get your free books now at
www.millsandboon.co.uk/freebookoffer

---

r fill in the form below and post it back to us

HE MILLS & BOON® BOOK CLUB™—HERE'S HOW IT WORKS: Accepting your
e books places you under no obligation to buy anything. You may keep the books
d return the despatch note marked 'Cancel'. If we do not hear from you, about a
onth later we'll send you 4 brand-new stories from the Modern™ series priced at
.30* each. There is no extra charge for post and packaging. You may cancel at any
e, otherwise we will send you 4 stories a month which you may purchase or return
us—the choice is yours. *Terms and prices subject to change without notice.
fer valid in UK only. Applicants must be 18 or over. Offer expires 28th February
12. **For full terms and conditions, please go to www.millsandboon.co.uk/
rmsandconditions**

---

rs/Miss/Ms/Mr (please circle)
_____

rst Name
_____

urname
_____

ddress
_____

_____

Postcode
_____

mail
_____

end this completed page to: Mills & Boon Book Club, Free Book
ffer, FREEPOST NAT 10298, Richmond, Surrey, TW9 1BR

Find out more at
www.millsandboon.co.uk/freebookoffer

*Visit us
Online*

0611/P1ZEE